Tara
and the
Man

Tara and the Man

Gary T. Brideau

iUniverse®

TARA AND THE MAN

iUniverse books may be ordered through booksellers or by contacting:

iUniverse
1663 Liberty Drive
Bloomington, IN 47403
www.iuniverse.com
1-800-Authors (1-800-288-4677)

ISBN: 978-1-5320-4091-7 (sc)
ISBN: 978-1-5320-4092-4 (e)

Print information available on the last page.

iUniverse rev. date: 01/12/2018

My thanks to
my sister, T. Jene Brideau, who started me writing
my wife who edits my stories

Story line

A level-headed Christian man, by the name of Ralph, meets a Christian woman by the name of Kathleen, who is hyped up, on pixies being real people. Ralph overlooked her enthusiasm for pixies and starts a relationship with her. One afternoon, while walking in the botanical garden Ralph discovers an injured Pixie and nurses her back to health.

Tara the Pixie, tells Ralph that Kathleen is nothing but a gold digger and will ruin his life. Things began to heat up when, the love-sick Pixie transforms herself into a normal woman, and makes plans to get Kathleen out of Ralph's life, and uncovers a plot to enslave the Pixies who live in a secret valley.

Chapter 1

THE MEETING

Ralph Walters, a medium built man, with short brown hair, in his late twenties, dressed in a light gray suit, walked out of church Sunday morning. Met Kathleen Summers, a well-built woman, with long wavy chestnut hair, in her mid-twenties, clad in a Topaz dress. She smiled at him and asked, "How long have you been going to this church?"

"I just started attending three weeks ago."

"You wanna go and get some ice cream?"

"My car or yours?"

"The ice cream parlor is just a couple of blocks from here. Take my hand and let's walk there."

In the ice cream parlor talking over two banana splits, Ralph asked, "Can I see you tomorrow?"

"I don't see why not. Make it one in the afternoon and we can take in a concert in the park. But first, you have to take me home."

Just then a short man clad in jeans and a t-shirt, with a scruffy beard sat at the table and asked, "Hey Kathleen. Who's the Poindexter?"

"He's a friend of mine so bug off Frank."

"You're giving me the brush off for him?"

"I already told you that I don't want to see you anymore."

"I can get you a job at Specialty Laboratories with a starting pay of twenty dollars an hour."

"Goodbye Frank."

Frank smiled, patted Kathleen's thigh, and said, "See ya around Doll Face."

Later, Ralph stood at Kathleen's front door gave her a long good night kiss and said, "I'll see you tomorrow."

"You wanna come in for a cup of coffee before you go?"

Three hours later, Ralph said good bye to Kathleen and walked to his car with thoughts of marriage on his mind.

A month into the relationship with Kathleen, she came to his apartment one afternoon clad in red slacks and a white top with a book entitled, 'Pixies, and Sprites, what are they?' Then told Ralph all about her enthusiasm over Pixies and that they were real people.

Ralph replied, "Whatever you want to call them they are mythical beings that the Swedish people made up years ago. Their word for them is pesky means wee little fairy. Besides, you do not find pixies in the Bible. They are fairy tales to tantalize the children."

"You make Pixies sound so dry and lifeless when in fact they are real. The degree of their intelligentsia is debatable though."

Two hours later, Kathleen told Ralph to take off his shirt and lie on his stomach on the floor. She then gave Ralph a long back rub that put him to sleep. An hour later, Ralph woke, with his sweetheart curled up beside him. Feeling frisky, Ralph kissed her lips, she woke, put her arms around him and kissed him back. forty-five minutes later, Kathleen sat up saying, "I am so sorry that I got carried away, have you seen my undies."

"It takes two you know. What we need to do right now is to get dressed, repent, and don't do it again."

After several months, Kathleen was talking to Ralph in his apartment and said, "I am sorry Hon, Frank forced his way into my home yesterday when I was in the shower and wanted to fool around. I opened the door and told him to leave or I would call the police."

"Did he do anything to you?"

"No. He left after I screamed and hollered rape."

"Did he ah?"

"Of course, not I am a Christian. There were times when I thought it was going to happen, but I maintained my walk with Christ."

"Why do you hang around that bum?"

"I thought I could win him to Christ. Boy, was I wrong with that idea. Hey, you wanna make out on the couch?"

"I don't know. The last time we kissed we almost got into sex."

"Alright then do you have any music by Bach?"

"Will Chopin do?"

"Sure will. Do you know how to waltz?"

"What's a waltz?"

"Take my hand and I will show you."

Ralph woke the next morning in bed with Kathleen snuggled against his side. He woke her and asked, "I thought you were going to go home last night? What are you doing in bed with me?"

"I was going to go home, but decided to give in to my desires, so I used the key you gave me, let myself back in and spend the night with you."

Ralph lifted the covers and asked, "Where are your clothes?"

"Take off your undies so we can spend some personal time together."

Two hours later, Ralph sat on the edge of the bed, Kathleen rubbed his back asked, "I'm a little wobbly on my feet can help me in the shower?"

"This is not what we are supposed to be doing as Christians and no I don't want to join you in the shower."

Three months later, Ralph proposed to Kathleen and the two of them went looking to buy a house. After months of searching, they decided to buy a colonial house in the country. Kathleen then stated, "If I take that job at Specialty Laboratories I can take some financial pressure off you."

"I don't like the idea of you being in contact with Frank again."

"I can handle myself around Frank. So, don't worry Sweetheart I am yours. Now, let's cuddle on the couch."

One evening several months after the house was purchased, Ralph stated, "Enough with the snuggle we have to start packing."

"I have to go home and get ready for work, I'll see you tomorrow."

Ralph held Kathleen by her shoulders and said, "Tell me that you are not seeing Frank again."

"Let me go and get rid of that jealousy of yours." snapped Kathleen.

"I am not jealous. A guy knows when there is something wrong with his Sweetheart. Now, what is It?"

"Nothing! I will see you tomorrow." and left.

Ralph sat in his recliner and said, "Lord Jesus. The spark has gone out of Kathleen's smile, and it has been replaced with a worried brow. The wanting to be with me she used to have, is now gone. What do I do? Go ahead with the marriage or call it off?"

Three days later, Kathleen entered Ralph's apartment and said, "Sorry I got tied up at work and couldn't get away. Here, let me give you a back rub."

An hour later, Ralph opened his eyes to see Kathleen's Pixie doll, Muf-Muf lying next to him. He sat up, held the doll and asked the doll, "Can you tell me what my Kathleen is up to these days? I thought so."

Kathleen's old friend Sally from high school poked her head in Ralph's open apartment door and shouted, "Anybody at home?"

"Come on in Sally."

"Where is Kathleen? She told me that she had the day off and I thought that she would be here helping you to pack. Oh well, give me a box and point me to a room."

Some hours later, Sally lay sprawled on the kitchen floor and said, "I must be out of shape. I'm bushed."

Ralph took off his shirt, sat on the floor next to her and asked, "You know Kathleen better than anyone. What is going on at work that I should know about?"

"Hasn't Kathleen told you?"

"Told me what?"

Sally stared at Ralph smiled sheepishly then said, "That the lab is offering a large reward for a Pixie."

"That's not what I meant. Is Kathleen hanging around Frank again?"

"I've seen her talking to him if that's what you mean." Sally sat behind Ralph and began to massage his back when Kathleen walked in and growled, "Well isn't this cozy. My best friend and my husband to be are fooling around on the kitchen floor."

Ralph stood up and said, "Get a grip on yourself will ya. I'm not gonna get into things with someone when the door is wide open. Sally was just rubbing my back which is something you haven't done in weeks. Now, how about carrying some boxes to my pickup so I can take a load to the house?"

"I guess I should if I want to keep an eye on you." growled Kathleen.

When Ralph went to the truck with an arm load of boxes. Sally saw a pair of men's white underwear in Kathleen's purse, pulled then out and whispered, "If you are going to cheat on Ralph. The least you could do is hide the evidence."

"I'm being forced into doing something that I don't want to do and don't know how to get out of of it."

"Grow a backbone Kathleen will ya, and walk away from Frank. Unless you want your marriage to go down the tubes."

Kathleen showed her friend the flyer that she had designed and asked, "Stan is looking for pixies. So, I designed this. What do you think?"

"With your knowledge of Pixies, I can see you cashing in on all that loot. By that way what does Stan want to do with a Pixie once he has them?"

"I don't know and I don't care. Hey, have you seen Ralph's 1943 copper penny?"

"He probably packed that long ago, and no I wasn't trying to get on with Ralph when you walked in. I worked too long and hard for my man Joe to blow it on an afternoon fling."

Ralph walked in and stated, "Are you girls gonna stand in the middle of the kitchen and jaw-jack? Or are you gonna help me?"

Ralph was alone in their new home for the first time with Kathleen, she changed into a halter top and hot pants, to finish unpacking the rest of the boxes. Ralph stared at the bruise just under her right breast and inquired, "Where did you get that nasty black and blue mark from?"

"I fell against something at work today."

Ralph thought, "That *looks more like somebody's fist than an object. Oh well, what do I know.*"

Kathleen asked, "Hey Hon, what did you do with your 1943 copper penny?"

"Who wants to know?"

"I do." stated Kathleen.

"It's in one of the boxes I packed."

"You wanna snuggle before you go home?"

"How about if I give you a back rub instead."

"That will work."

A few minutes into the back massage, Ralph was asleep. Kathleen then searched his pockets and some of the boxes muttering, "Stan wants me to find that penny, to support his new project."

Ralph woke forty minutes later his stomach, felt Kathleen's bare side against him and said, "It's not going to happen Sweetheart. We should wait until after we are married to get into things. Make yourself decent and I'll put on a pot of coffee."

An hour later, Ralph poured the coffee, Kathleen closed her bathrobe, smiled, and said, "Admit it, you can't say no to me, so where is the penny?"

"Can we talk about what just happened."

"Are you upset with me because I pushed your buttons to get you to respond to me."

"Yes, and don't do it again."

Chapter 2

THERE ARE NO PIXIES

Ralph was clad in jean cut-offs and a t-shirt as he walked out of a rustic looking colonial home that sat on three acres of woodland. He turned to Kathleen, who was dressed in topaz Bermuda shorts, and a white top. Ralph gave her a peck on the cheek. Then stated, "Will you look at that sky. Not a cloud to be seen, the perfect day for move in our new home."

"I'll be moving in after we are married. But, what are we gonna do with all that junk the previous owners left in the basement?"

"We might be able to sell the ranch, dollhouse, along with the doll clothes and that heavy black plastic in a tag sale."

"I was looking at our huge deck out back Kathleen, what do you say we put up some realistic looking pixies? I have all the material and the time. I think it would look so cool."

"Pixies, pixy, pizkie, paslies, sprites, whatever you want to call them they are mythical beings that the Swedish people made up, and their word for them is pesky, means wee little fairy. Besides, do you not find Pixies in the Bible?"

"Yeah, yeah, yeah, you've told me the history of Pixies hundreds of times, why don't you just tell me that you don't want me to put them on the deck."

"Go ahead do what you want, just don't expect me to like them. Now, let's get the pickup truck unpacked because the moving van will be here any minute."

That evening, Ralph made a fire in the fireplace, placed two meatball subs on a tablecloth that he spread on the brown carpet and said, "Coffee will be along any minute."

Kathleen scanned the walls in the living room and stated, "You know. I think this room would look a whole lot better if it was topaz along with the dining room off the living room. What do you think?"

"Fine with me. You wanna paint the spare bedroom downstairs light blue?"

"Nah. A deep blue would look better."

"Don't tell me you want to put pixies in there too."

"I wasn't thinking of it but that is a splendid idea."

After Ralph took his shirt off and made-out with Kathleen in front of the fireplace. She put her blouse back on, rolled him on his stomach and began to rub his shoulders saying, "If there are things walking around this planet called Sasquatch. Then there must be a diminutive group of people with wings living somewhere on this planet."

"You do have a point. However, if you keep this up I'm gonna be asleep in no time."

Ralph woke the next morning on the living room floor, with a one-foot tall pixie doll looking at him, leaning against a pillow. He was about to throw it out the sliding glass door, but thought, *"Better not,"* and placed it on the mantle over the fireplace.

Seven minutes later, the home phone rang. He answered it saying, "Hey Babe. You coming over today? There is plenty of boxes to unpack."

"Sorry, Hon. my friend Sally from high school is coming over and we are going to spend the day shopping. Oh, did Muf-Muf wake you this morning?"

"Who or what is a Muf-Muf?"

"You remember, it's my little pixie pay. I sat her on the floor by you to keep you company."

Ralph sighed then said, "Kathleen, when are you going to learn that pixies don't exist and I wish you wouldn't stick them in my face like that."

"I'm just trying to get you to see the possibility that pixies do exist."

"Pixies, sprites, fares, leprechauns, wee people, you can put them in the same category as Big Foot."

"Sorry I can't debate you on this subject right now Hon, because I have to meet Sally in a few minutes, love you."

Ralph hung up the phone muttering to himself, "When is that woman going to pull her head out of the clouds and stop talking about pixies. It's just not healthy for a grown woman."

A week later, Ralph unpacked the last box, called Kathleen, and asked, "Where have you been? You were supposed to help me unpack."

"Sorry Hon, Sally and I were so busy talking about old times. But, I'll be there first thing tomorrow morning."

"You are a day late and a dollar short, I just finished."

"What do you say I meet you tomorrow at one o'clock in the Botanical garden in the center of town?"

"Alright, what part?"

"There is a bench by the patch of Sweet Williams. Meet me there at one o'clock."

Three minutes after one the next day, Ralph stood by the patch of pink Sweet Williams, glanced at his watch, muttering, "Where is Kathleen? I Pray she is not going to stand me up again."

Suddenly, something glanced off his right shoulder then landed in the patch of flowers, followed by a robin that almost slammed him in his head. Ralph looked around wondering what was happening. Then muttered, "Stupid birds."

He then heard faint moaning coming from the Sweet Williams that caught his attention. He knelt, parted the flowers, and saw a one-foot tall female Pixie with short black hair and a few dark red rags for clothing. Ralph mumbled, "That can't be a real pixie, it has to be some kids doll or Kathleen is playing games with me again." Ralph picked up the doll and thought, *"Hey wait a minute this is a real pixie. But, it can't be they are not supposed to be real."* Ralph looked around, quickly unbuttoned his shirt, and gently placed it inside, called Kathleen saying, "Sorry Babe, something came up and I can't meet you in the garden today."

"Then we'll do it tomorrow."

"Ahhh, I think I am coming down with something. So, why don't we meet next week when I am feeling better."

"I can come over tomorrow with some soup."

"Thanks,"

Ralph hurried home, placed the unconscious pixie on a folded hand towel on the kitchen counter, removed her rags, and cleaned her up. Then went in the basement, dug up the doll clothes, put a pair of pink Pjs on her, then placed her on a single bed in the bedroom on the first floor and covered her with a red linen napkin.

All that night, Ralph tended to his tiny guest making sure she was comfortable, wiping her forehead with a cold wet cloth.

As the first rays of the morning light shown through the bedroom window, the pixie placed her hand on her head and muttered in Irish Gaelic. "Cad a Popper ceann a bhí." stared at Ralph and hollered, "Whoa! Duine! Cá ndeachaigh tú teacht ó?" She then she went to fly, but fell to the floor screaming in pain.

Ralph went to pick her up but she scurried under the bed terrified of what he was going to do to her. Ralph lay on the floor and said, "I am not going to hurt you."

"So you say, Human."

"If I was going to harm you I would have done it while you were unconscious."

"You have a point Creep. But cad eile a rinne tú dom?"

"In English please."

"What else did you do to me while I was passed out, Creep?"

"I took off your rags, cleaned you up, then put those Pjs on you. That's all. Now, can we be friends?"

"I guess so. But, this is so weird making friends with a human. Okay, human help me up because I can't move me right wing."

Ralph picked up the pixie and inquired, "Do you have a name?"

The pixie struggled to stand, bowed saying, "I am known as Tara."

"Glad to meet you, Tara, I am Ralph."

"Could you put a hot cloth on my back because my back hurts?"

"Sure, I'll bring you into the kitchen, place you on a hand towel, and apply a hot compress."

In the kitchen, Tara stood on the counter, looked up at Ralph and said, "If you will excuse me I have to cover me cíocha."

"What's a cíocha?"

"Just turn your back until I say it's okay."

With Tara lying face down on a hand towel on the kitchen counter,

Ralph placed a warm paper towel on the pixie's back. then asked, "Do you want to tell me why you did a face plant in that flowerbed?"

"I was trying to find my way back to Little Ireland when this bird tried to make a snack of me. I would have eluded him but some dumb human stepped in my way. That's when the lights went out and the next thing I am looking at you. Do you know how frightening it is to open your eye to see a giant staring you in the face? If you will pardon me language. You scared the crap out of me."

"Sorry. It won't happen again."

"It better not or I'll kick your sorry butt all over this house if it does."

"Big talk for a small fry."

"I had to be tough when I was growing up or I would have died."

"Would my lady like some tea and a muffin?"

"I sure would."

Ralph made a pot of tea, placed it on the dining room table. Put a dolls cup and saucer in front of Tara. Then sat a large blueberry muffin between them. Tara stared at the muffin that came up to her middle with her mouth open in shock. Then stated, "I'm sorry but I am not used to seeing so much food in all my life."

"Dig in. There is plenty to go around."

Tara ripped off a chunk muffin, sat down to drink her tea. Thirteen minutes later, Tara lay on her back and moaned, "I don't believe I made a pig of myself with that muffin."

Ralph stared at Tara and stated, "I don't believe I am sitting at my dining room table having tea with a pixie. How weird is that?"

"Just as weird as having a human for a friend."

"Are you up for me to show you my home?"

"As long as I can sit on your shoulder."

Ralph placed his hand on the table, Tara walked up his arm and sat on his shoulder.

Forty-five minutes later, Ralph walked downstairs saying, "That little lady is my home."

"What is down below?"

"You mean in the basement?"

"Yeah, that's the place. What's down there?"

"Just a lot of junk."

11

"I want to see, I want to see."

In the basement, Ralph stopped at a pile of junk in the upper left-hand corner and said, "This is it, junk"

"What's in that brown paper bag on our left?"

Ralph opened it saying, "Just a bunch baskets and fake flowers."

"Ohhh, pretty. I have an idea. Why don't you use them to decorate the top of the kitchen cabinets? You hand them to me one at a time, and I'll arrange them."

"Great. Let's go for it."

Fifty minutes later, Tara stood on Ralph's right shoulder, studied the floral arrangement, and said, "Not bad if I do say so myself."

Later, Ralph stood in front of the fireplace, put his hand on the mantle saying, "Walk up my arm to the mantle and look at Kathleen's picture then tell me what do you think of her?"

Tara stood in front of an eight and a half by eleven picture of Kathleen and asked, "Is she the one who captured your heart?"

"Oh yeah."

"I don't like her. She has shifty eyes, and a mean look too. Nope, I don't like her."

"Kathleen is a lover of pixies."

"And you are going somewhere with that statement?"

"No. I guess not." Ralph glanced at his watch and said, "It's getting late. Why don't I fix you up a box, put it on my nightstand so you can sleep in it?"

Tara placed her hands on her hips saying, "Really. Do I look like a puppy dog to you?"

"Ah no. Do you have any suggestions?"

"Sure do. Fold up a hand towel, place it on your nightstand, then fold a washcloth for a pillow. I'll crawl between the folds of the towel and sleep."

"How is your back doing?"

"I'm glad you asked, I need another heat treatment before beddy-bye."

Thirteen minutes later, Ralph stared at Tara fast asleep, placed some doll clothes on the nightstand for her then crawled in bed.

The next morning, Tara put on her light blue slacks and matching top, hopped on the bed. then walked up Ralph's chest, lifted his right eyelid and asked, "Hello! You awake? It's past seven."

"I am now. I'll have breakfast in a bit." Ralph threw back the covers, placed his feet on the floor. Tara, stared at Ralph, covered her eyes shouting, "Help, my eyes my eyes I can't see!"

"Is there anything I can do?"

"Yes. Please get rid of those Pjs!"

"What's wrong with them? Kathleen picked them out for me."

"That figures. I have never seen a bunch of confused pattern of red, yellows, greens, and blues in all my life. So, for the sake of this Pixie's eyesight dump them in the trash."

Before Ralph had his top unbuttoned, Tara threw up her hand shouting, "Hold on there human, let this pixie leave the room first!"

"I'm going across the hall for a shower, then I make breakfast. Okay?"

Chapter 3

TARA TAKES A STAND

After Ralph had his shower, Tara patiently sat on a coffee can watching him cook three eggs sunny side up, three strips of bacon and toast a raisin bagel. He then set the dining room table for one, placed a doll's table and chair on the table and a set small plate and eating utensils, then sat down.

Tara sat at her table and hollered, "Hey, what about me? I need to eat too!"

Ralph pointed to his plate saying, "Pick up your plate and help yourself. Or I could cook you up your own bacon and egg if you like."

"Thank you but it would take me a month of Sundays just to eat it. I'll take some of yours, if you don' mind." Tara took enough from Ralph's plate to fill her stomach.

Just then, the front doorbell rang, Ralph, glanced at his watch and said, "Kathleen is here, Wow it's that late already? Tara, why don't you hide in that Boston Fern in the living room."

Ralph opened the door and said with a smile, "Kathleen, my you are looking exceptionally alert today."

Kathleen stared at Ralph then inquired, "Okay, what did you break?"

"Nothing. I thought a compliment would be nice."

"Are you seeing another woman behind my back?"

"No, why would I do something like that to the most wonderful lady in the world."

"Now I know you are up to something. Who is she?"

"Alright, you got me. She is the cutest thing I have ever seen and she is all of one-foot high."

"Have I told you how precious you are to me. Hey, where is my welcome kiss?"

"Sorry." Ralph kissed Kathleen, glancing at the fern to make sure Tara wasn't trying to sneak a peek at his girlfriend.

Kathleen ordered, "Here are the keys, get the paint and stuff in the trunk. I figure we paint the downstairs bedroom first. I'll set up the room while you change into the disposable coveralls I bought."

Late that evening, Ralph finished painting the bedroom, hallway, living- room and dining room. Ralph gazed at his wife to be and asked, "How is it that you don't have a speck of paint on you?"

"Like I told you. I set the room up and you paint."

"Hon, can I see your hands?"

"Sure. See."

Ralph promptly painted her hands topaz, saying, "You can't paint without getting some on you."

"Ralph Walters," hollered Kathleen, "What did you do that for?"

"I could have painted your face like this." Ralph then touched the right side of her face with the paintbrush. Kathleen wiped her hands-on Ralph. He glanced down at the plastic covering the floor, picked up the paint can that was one eight full, walked to Kathleen, smiled. She put her hands up saying, Ralph F. Walters, you wouldn't dare pour that paint over my head."

"You are right I am not. He hooked his index finger on the front of her blouse, pulled and poured it down inside her top. She let go a scream, "Noooo!" Then stood still as the paint made its way down her stomach, and legs to fill her loafers.

Ralph stared at Kathleen standing in the middle of the dining room, dripping with paint, her face red with anger and thought, "I am so dead for doing that."

Kathleen smiled devilishly, wrapped her arms around Ralph and gave him a hug and asked, "How do you like being full of paint? After all, Turnabout is fair play."

Ralph inquired, "I have just one question, "How are you going to get to the bathroom to shower and change?"

"I don't know. You have just as much paint on you as I do."

Ralph stepped out of his coveralls, took off his shoes and socks saying, "I always wear a t-shirt and a Bermuda shorts underneath paint coveralls. I'll lay down some plastic so you can get to the bathroom. Then, I'll get your change of clothes from my room."

"Could you wash my back?" Inquired Kathleen, feeling kittenish.

"No, that would be wrong and you know it."

While his fiancé was showering, Ralph knelt by the fern, parted it, and asked, "How are you doing Tara? You need something to put in your stomach?"

"You like the red on my lips?"

Ralph looked closer then asked, "Where did you get lipstick from?"

"Kathleen's purse. You should see what else she has in there."

"I am not interested in her personal belongings, and you say out of her pocketbook."

"You wouldn't stay that if you saw the sexy photo she had of a hunk called Frank."

Kathleen stood by the bathroom door wrapped in her towel, listening to Ralph for a minute before asked, "Why are you talking to that Boston Fern?"

Ralph quickly spun around, smiling sheepishly, and said, "Soft words help it to grow but this one happens to be stubborn."

"Cut it out will ya Ralph you're scaring me."

Kathleen picked up her purse, to put on some makeup and questioned, "Where is my lipstick and powder compact?"

"Did you leave them home?" Ralph glanced at the fern, saw Tara waving at him giggling, he shook his finger at her. She then rolled the lipstick and powder compact on the floor, Ralph picked it up and said, "It must have fallen out."

"If I didn't know any better I'd say that a pixie was playing pranks on me."

"Now, you are scaring me. You know that they don't exist."

"You wanna kiss for a while?" asked Kathleen.

"With you in just a towel, that would be dangerous."

"Party popper."

After Kathleen was dressed, Ralph put on some Chopin, lit a fire in the fireplace and said, "Sit and rest Sweetheart." Ralph glanced at the fern, saw Tara waltzing around with a smile on her face, then pointed to him. Ralph shook his head then motioned for her to hide on the fern.

Kathleen glanced at Ralph, then at the fern then asked, "What is it about that fern? You've been fussing over it all evening. There is a sprite in it isn't there." Kathleen walked to the fern and diligently searched every inch of it. While Ralph stood behind her praying that she would not find Tara. He then said, "The coffee is ready, the fire is warm and the music is soft and low. All I need right now is you."

Buffalo fetters!" growled Kathleen, "I could have sworn there was a pixie in that fern. Oh well next time"

Kathleen snuggled up to Ralph by the fire listening to Chopin for an hour then she asked, "Hon, can you take off your shirt? I want to give you a back rub before I leave."

Tara poked her head out of the fern and watching the expression of pleasure on Ralph's face as Kathleen rubbed his back. She then folded her arms across her chest and pouted. Thinking, "*There isn't enough room in Ralph's life for the two of us, so, Kathleen has to go.*"

In the morning, Tara took the pixie doll Muf-Muf that Kathleen had put to watch over Ralph and dragged it away. Then sat watching Ralph sleeping. When she thought that he should be up, she lifted one of his eyelids, looked at him saying, "Wakey, wakey."

Ralph sat up and moaned, "It's morning already. I have got to stop sleeping on the floor because it is not doing my back any good."

Tara climbed on Ralph's lap, shook her finger at him saying, "If I were bigger I would have been by your side helping you paint instead of giving you orders."

"Kathleen isn't bossy and you need to be more careful that she doesn't see you until I have the chance to introduce you. And what do you mean by accusing Kathleen of seeing another guy behind my back."

"Well, she is. take a look." Tara dragged out a snapshot of Frank posing in a speed-o bathing suit. Ralph turned it over and read, To my main squeeze, Kathleen." Ralph glanced at Tara and stated, "It's most likely an old photo she forgot she had in her purse. No big deal."

Tara climbed on Ralph's left shoulder and stated, "Don't you turn a blind eye to something that will cause you hurt in the future. Hey, look at me when I'm talking to you, Mister!"

Ralph smiled, saying, "You have a lot of spunk for someone who is only twelve inches tall. Oh, and that red lipstick looks good on you. Now for breakfast."

At breakfast, Ralph had the same meal setup as before, Tara took a bite of her egg and said, "This is so cool eating like this with you. Oh, you know that huge shower stall you have on the first floor. Have you ever thought about turning it into an indoor pool? All you would have to do is put something in the doorway."

"Clever idea."

That morning, Ralph found a piece of aluminum that would fit in the shower doorway. Secured it to the door then filled the shower stall with four feet of water. He then found a three-foot square piece of wood for Tara to use. Put on his skimpy spedo bathing suit and relaxed in the warm water.   Tara dressed in a two-piece bathing suit stated, "My, don't we look sexy." she then climbed on Ralph's shoulder hollered, "Can Cannonball!" and leaped.

While Ralph was floating on his back, Tara climbed on his chest, lay down on her stomach looked at Ralph and stated, "Isn't this better than a boring shower. She then kissed him on his chin.

Ralph picked up the frisky pixie, stood up saying, "That's enough for one day. I have to get on my computer and earn some money so I can pay the bills."

In the den, Tara sat on a stack of sticky note pads and watched Ralph work on his computer. When he left to get himself a drink of water. Tara logged onto a website and ordered a special brand of herbs and spices then went back to the web page Ralph was working on.

Late that afternoon, Ralph called Kathleen and asked, "So, how has your day been?"

"Fair to middlyn. Why do you ask?"

"By any chance do you know a guy by the name of Frank?"

"You know I do. He's just a friend that I meet for coffee, share burdens of the day, talk about other stuff. Why do you want to know?"

"I found his picture on the living room floor this morning. Which made me doubt our relationship."

"I am not marrying him, Hon. He is just a good friend that I go out to coffee with."

"I don't like the idea of you seeing him again. We are engaged to be married."

"There is nothing wrong with me seeing Frank, it is not like we are into things we shouldn't. So, don't worry I know what I am doing."

"That was Peggy Marsh's last words just before she told her husband that she was expecting the guys baby. When a man and a woman are serious about each other. They stop seeing their friends of the opposite sex. Because things can happen."

"No, they won't."

"You are a woman and have feelings that can be stirred up by a man so it is wrong for you to be seeing him."

"Ralph, I don't want to talk about this anymore. I will see you tomorrow afternoon."

"What. After you see Frank."

"Goodbye Ralph."

Ralph stared at Tara, put his head down, and walked out on the back deck to be alone.

Four hours later, Ralph opened the sliding glass door, saw Tara on the kitchen counter and grumbled, "You were right."

"Don't shut me out like that again. I may be a foot tall but I still can comfort you. Can I give you a hug?" The pixie flew up to Ralph, put her arms around his neck and asked, "There, feel better?"

Ralph smiled saying, "You are one of a kind you know that. I just wish you were my size. The places we could go and the fun we could have. But, that will never happen."

"Hey, can I give you a back rub?"

"How is a little thing like you going to do that?"

"Give me a chance to prove myself."

"Alright."

Ralph removed his shirt and pants, thinking, *"She's just a pixie no need to be modest."* He lay on the floor by the fireplace then waited. Tara dragged a tube of cream on Ralph's back, opened it then jumped on it sending a good amount of cream all over Ralph's back. She then proceeded to apply it.

An hour later, Tara got in Ralph's face, wiped her hands on his cheeks and asked, "What do you think? Do I get the job?"

"You did a wonderful job."

Tara's wings fluttered as she kissed Ralph on his lower lip." Then lie on the lower part of his stomach and went to sleep.

Chapter 4

TARA TO THE RESCUE

That evening, Ralph put Tara on the mahogany brown end table next to the couch, sat and stated, "I chewed out Kathleen for seeing another man and I'm doing the same with you. I am sorry for letting you see me in my underwear."

"You are helping an injured sprite. Besides, there is a difference in dating and helping someone you know and don't worry if I see you in your undies."

"I noticed you flew which means you are free to go."

Tara twisted her left wing on an angle saying, "I, ah, blew out my left wing when I flew. So, can I stay just a few more days?"

"I guess so. But, we need to set up different arrangements other than you sleeping on my nightstand."

"What's wrong with that? I wake you first thing in the morning, we make breakfast together, I love it. I just wish I was bigger so I could help you."

"For one, I need my privacy. Two, we should not be sharing the same room. You may be twelve inches tall but, you are still a woman and it is not right for you to see me in my underwear."

"I don't mind. However, I'm just a little Pixie what can I do? So, stop worrying how you're dressed around me."

"Okay. but from now on, I'll use the master bedroom upstairs this way you can stay in this room."

Tara stamped her foot saying, "Drats! That means I can't wake you in the morning."

"It's not right for the two of us to be in the same bedroom."

Tara lowered her head saying, "Oh, alright, if that's the way you want it, I'll go along with your decision. I don't like it, but hopefully, you will change your mind."

Ralph placed a Bible on his lap saying, "We need to discuss this."

"Done that. Didn't like it."

"I am going to read from the Psalms today."

"I'm outta here."

Ralph placed his hand over Tara so she could not move saying, "Hold on there, Short Point. Part of the house rules are, daily devotions is a must. So, park that little bottom of yours and listen."

A half hour later, Ralph stated, "That wasn't so bad, was it?"

"No."

Just then the doorbell rang, Ralph answered it, then sat the eight-inch square brown box in front of the pixie and said, "Are you, Tara M. Walters?"

Tara cringed and said, "It came Yes! Sorry I used your last name to order something."

"What is it?"

"I can't tell you right now, but, it is something that will make the two of very happy."

"Where do you want me to put it?"

"In my room but don't open it."

Ralph stared at Tara then muttered "I know how to solve the sleeping problem." he went into the basement, cleaned out three-quarters of it. Covered it with heavy black plastic, then built a stone wall two feet high to close off that section of the basement. He brought in good planting soil and filled that part of the basement with it.

Then, in the back-left corner, Ralph built a mountain seven and a half feet high with a waterfall that ran down into a large pool, then scattered small shrubs around the mountain. Ralph landscaped around the falls with rolled grass, then planted flowers, bushes, and trees that resembled a patch of woods in the basement. Finally, Ralph rounded off the ceiling, painted it blue like the sky and put in plant lighting to keep everything growing. He stood watching the water cascade over the rock and into the pool and thought, "*That should make Tara happy. But why do I feel like there is something is missing? Ah. Yes. The house.*" Ralph fastened the large dollhouse to the wall on the left side of the *falls, smiled and said,* "That's it."

Ralph went upstarts, quickly picked up Tara saying, "That's it Half Point. You are living in the basement from here on in and I don't want any of your lip."

"You can't banish me down there with all the spiders and creepy things. I protest my rights as a pixie are being violated!"

Ralph put Tara in a paper lunch bag saying, "This is it, so, quiet for now."

Tara beat the inside of the bag hollering and screaming in protest but wore herself out instead.

In the basement by the falls, Ralph carefully placed the bag on the soft green grass, then said, "You can come out now."

The Bag fell on its side, as Tara crawled out, grumbling, "I will never forgive you if I get eaten by a spider." She stood up, stared at the falls then slowly scanned the transformed basement with her mouth opened in shock.

Ralph smiled and asked, "Do you like your new home? It's all yours."

Tara flew up to Ralph threw her arms around his throat thanking him repeatedly.

Ralph inquired. "Why don't you check out your house?"

"My house?" I have a home too?"

"You sure do. It's right over there."

Tara fluttered down, slowly opened the front door and entered. She came out thirteen minutes later and said, "I love the wallpaper, bedroom, the shower. Everything works. It's like someone built it just for me."

"I wanted you to be happy during your stay."

Tara stared at the falls, then said, "But that thing you call a pixie that's sitting on the mountain is wearing my bathing suit."

"Oh, that's Muf-Muf, and if you look close enough you will find holes and cracks where you can hide just in case somebody comes down here."

"You mean like Kathleen."

"Exactly. But why do you need a bathing suit inside?"

"Good point. Hey, wait a minute, you stuck pixies all over the place. I must admit they do look a little creepy, but lifelike. But why are you trying to make me feel at home?"

"Kathleen will want to know why I built all of this. So, with all the phony sprites around I have an excuse. Oh, that box on the left side of the house has all your clothes in it."

Tara pointed and asked, "There is a hole in the ceiling by that tall tree. What's it for?"

"It used to be a laundry shut. But now it is your personal access to the first and second floor. That is when your wings are healed."

Tara put a forlorn expression on her face and asked, "Could you please give me a back rub? My wings are sore."

"Okay, lie on the grass and I'll take care of you. Just don't take anything off."

"I wouldn't think of it." stated Tara giggling softly to herself.

Ralph lay on his side and used his index finger to rub Tara's back. She groaned, "Ohhhh yeahhhh. Don't even think of stopping. Can you rub, just under my right Scapula, that's it, now rub my Coccyx?"

Ralph smiled and asked, "Are you sure you want me to rub down there?" As Ralph touched Tara's tailbone, he heard, "Ralph Walters! What in God's name have you done to the basement?"

"Shoot, that's Kathleen I left the front door unlocked, quick hide in the caves."

Tara did a short hop to the falls and hid in the cave just as Kathleen appeared from behind a large bush in a yellow sundress. Then inquired, "Are you trying to get on my good side? If you are you just did. Tell me one thing. What possessed you to do all this?"

"If you will look at the falls, Muf-Muf is enjoying herself on the mountain."

"So, she is, but you haven't answered my question. Why?"

"If you catch a pixie or a sprite, you can keep it here. What's in the bag?"

"I brought us coffee and doughnuts."

After Kathleen took off Ralph's shirt, she pushed him on his back kissed him and asked, "You wanna cuddle for a while?"

As Kathleen snuggled up to Ralph on the grass, she let out a scream, grabbed her leg saying, "Something just bit me."

"Are you sure? There is nothing down here that will bite you unless it was a spider."

"Trust me, that was no spider. Anyways, I want to rub your back."

Ralph lay on his stomach, Kathleen put on surgical gloves, then rubbed a white cream with a sedative mixed in it on his back. Within a minute, Ralph was asleep. She then, placed Muf-Muf a foot from Ralph's face and went upstairs.

Kathleen called Frank and said, "I dragged Ralph so it is alright for you to come over."

"What if he wakes?"

"Do I have to remind you that Muf-Muf has a device in her that will signal me if he moves."

Ten minutes later, Frank walked in, gave Kathleen a passionate kiss on her lips then stated, "I don't know about you, but I am going to use the saps shower before we look for the ring and 1943 copper penny, if he has it."

"Let me know when you are finished so I can give you a body rub, and trust me Ralph has the penny and ring because he showed them to me the other day."

"Did he put in a safety deposit box?

"No, just take your shower."

Later, while Kathleen sat at the counter drinking her coffee, Frank walked up behind her, in Ralph's robe, put his arms around her gave her a passionate kiss and asked, "What is that you are reading?"

"It's my ad from Specialty Laboratories saying that they will pay $85.000.00 dollars to the first person who will bring them a pixie. But I want to get my hands on one pixie in particular."

"That's a laugh."

"Hey, they're out there somewhere and I plan to find one then cash in on all that loot. Now start searching and whatever you do, don't make a mess."

"Hold on there just a minute, we are in this together. You either help me or I don't search."

While the two were arguing, Tara was listening from the laundry shut, and thought, *"I know where that penny is along with a diamond ring."* Tara flew up the laundry-shut to the second floor, flew in the master bedroom to the men's jewel box on the bureau, opened it. Put the ring around her neck and held the penny in her hands then flew back down the shoot to hide them in the cave. She then flew back up the shut to watch.

Kathleen had just finished giving Frank a back rub and he was putting on Ralph's robe. Kathleen went to the bureau with Frank, opened the jewel box and exclaimed, "Dang! They are not here! The three-carat diamond ring and penny has to be in this bedroom somewhere!"

"Are you sure?

"Yes!"

"I'll take the closest you look in all the drawers."

Kathleen stared at Frank in Ralph's robe and said, "Take off that robe and get dressed before Ralph wakes and catches you."

"Right now, Sweet Cheeks?"

"Yes, Now."

Tara flew into the kitchen, tore off a piece of sponge, shoved several sewing needles in it then went back upstairs and hid behind the nightstand. Just as Kathleen was about to sit on the bed with Frank, Tara threw the sponge. Kathleen screamed in pain and fell on the floor crying for help. Frank raced in the bedroom, removed the needles saying, "Will you please watch where you are sitting. Do you want me to bandage your booboo?"

"Can the sick humor and find the penny and ring."

Tara snuck under the bed and climbed in the box-spring so she wouldn't be discovered. But could not resist playing one more prank on them. Tara followed the two into the dining room and darted under the table, and waited until and Kathleen sat at the table. She tied Frank's shoelaces together then hid up under the chair. When Frank went to stand, he fell to the floor with a crash, Kathleen shouted, "Ralph, are you alright?"

Frank quickly hobbled out the door as Ralph charged upstairs saying, "Kathleen, do you want me to call 911?"

"I'll be fine. Just being clumsy tonight, I guess. I see you are awake. Is there anything I can do for you? Coffee, pie?"

Ralph spotted Tara trying to sneak away, grabbed Kathleen, held her tight and began kissing her. Then with one eye opened he watched Tara fly down the hall.

Eleven minutes later, Kathleen broke from Ralph saying, "That's a switch."

You are never the one to start the kissing."

"I thought a change would spark some life into our relationship."

"You did more than that. Come here tiger, you are mine." and pulled him on the floor.

Twenty minutes later, Ralph, placed his hand over Kathleen's mouth and said, "I think that is enough for one night."

"Ah come on I want you." pawing at his clothes.

Ralph sat up then said, "I said, no."

"Now you are being a killjoy."

"No. I am keeping us from doing something that we will be sorry for in the morning."

Then why did you lead me on if you were not interested in doing anything more than kissing."

Ralph stared at Kathleen in shock then asked, "Didn't we make an agreement to keep our relationship out of the flesh? Then why do you want to go against it?"

Kathleen put her head down and said, "I am sorry Ralph. It is just that I'm not used to you being so rambunctious, it made me want more and I lost control. Sorry. Hey, it's getting late, I'll call you in a few days."

"What's wrong with tomorrow?"

"Mom wants me to help her plant some flowers in her garden and you know Mom when she gets in her gardening mood."

"Yeah." stated Ralph, gave Kathleen a peck on the cheek and escorted her to the door.

Ralph entered the bathroom that had the large shower stall. Studied the four feet of water, glanced at the door, stepped out of his clothes and into the water to relax muttering, "I should turn this into a giant jacuzzi. I have the money."

"That's a great idea," stated Tara." sitting on the piece of aluminum that was across the doorway.

"Hey, you are, not supposed to be in here."

"You look comfortable. Can I join you?"

"Definitely no."

"Why not? We did it before."

Ralph stared at Tara, glanced down.

She smiled sheepishly said, "Oh, Sorry."

"Get me my trunks then you can join me."

Chapter 5

DECIDED LOVE

The next morning, Tara sat at her table enjoying her breakfast, glanced at Ralph, smiled sheepishly and said "I am so sorry for barging in on you yesterday. I had no idea that you were relaxing in your altogether."

Ralph took a bite of his strawberry pancake, stared at Tara and said, "No problem, but, you are not being completely honest with me. Are you?"

Tara kept her head down as she stated, "The way you made these small pancakes for me is really fantastic, thank you."

"Don't change the subject. You know what I'm talking about. So out with it."

In mock innocence, Tara stated, "I haven't been lying to you about anything, honest."

"Then let me spell it out for you. Actions speak louder than words. You act as if your wings are incapacitated. But, I know there is nothing wrong with your wings. From one friend to the next, you can tell me why you want to hang around me instead of being with your sprite friends. Did the other sprites kick you out of their community because you did something wrong?"

"I'm too embarrassed to tell you, so when I finished my breakfast I'll go elsewhere to live."

Ralph studied Tara's ruby red lips, her neatly brushed hair, her white blouse, and baby blue skirt paused and said, "I was too busy nursing you back to health to see that you are in love with me."

Tara's lower lip quivered as she stated, "I didn't plan for it to happen but you make me feel so special and wanted, that I fell in love with you. All I'll ask of you is this, that you bring me back to the botanical gardens and I'll be on my way."

"I'm sorry I can't do that because I've grown attached to you also."

Tara's face lit up as she asked, "Then I can stay? She rose to her feet and ask, "Ralph, can you put your face down to my level? I need to do something."

Ralph leaned forward, then lowered his face to 8 inches above the table, Tara walked up to him and kissed his lower lip. He straightened up picked up Tara and kissed her face, then put her back down.

Tara was so flustered that she tripped and fell face first in the butter dish.

Ralph sat her on her feet, and chuckled, "You need to watch where you are going."

"Dang! I just put this outfit on too. Now, I have to go downstairs, shower and change."

"The kitchen sink is deep enough so nothing important will show. Why don't I fill that with nice sudsy water and you can bathe there? I won't peek."

"Works for me. I'll go for it. Oh, I think I have a pair of slacks and a top in the nightstand in the first-floor bedroom."

Twenty minutes later, Ralph walked up to the kitchen sink, watched Tara splashing around and said, "For a short point you sure make a mess. Ready to come out?"

Tara climbed out, sat on the edge of the sink, and wrapped a facecloth around saying, "Thanks, that was fun. Can you do me a favor and dry my back?"

"I think I can do that."

Tara stood, handed Ralph the washcloth, and turned around, saying, "Don't push too hard on my back. Ohhh, that feels good. But you didn't have to dry my legs and thighs too."

"I have to take care of my little lady."

Ralph handed Tara her clothes saying, "I noticed you don't have any underwear. You like to go commando?"

"That is so gross. They don't make foundation garments in my size, so I am stuck going commando."

"I think I have the remedy for that. Tara, before you put your blouse on, I want to take a look at your wing muscles."

The pixie stood back too on the counter with her arms folded across her chest, and asked, "What's wrong? Do I have wing blight?"

"No. But your black blue around your wings so, I'd cool it on the flying for a few days."

"Yes, Doc. Now, can I put my clothes on?"

Later, in Ralph's car, he fastened the seat belt, Tara slid under it and inquired, "Where are we going? You are aware that I can't let human's see me."

"I think this one you can."

Twenty minutes later, Ralph parked his car in the driveway of an English cottage, unbuttoned the last button of his green shirt and instructed Tara to climb in. As he was buttoned his shirt, Tara coughed and gagged then asked,

"Have you smelled yourself lately? It stinks in here."

"Can the comic routine and be quiet unless you want to be found out."

Ralph knocked on the front door and said, "Emma. It's me, Ralph Walters."

A spry elderly woman with snow white hair opened the door, saying, "I'm not that old that you have to tell me who you are. Come in, come in. I just took a batch of scones out of the over."

"A cup of your spice tea would hit the spot."

Emma served Ralph his tea and scones then said, "Wait till I show you my latest work." Emma placed twelve pairs of small shoes on the table and asked, "What do you think? They are made from genuine leather with laces."

"But, why Grammy Emma?"

"I figure that one-day pixies will come to me for supplies. So, I want to be ready when they do."

Ralph placed Tara on the table, she smiled at her and waved.

Emma's mouth and eyes opened wide in surprise as she stared at the pixie standing in front of her. Then questioned, "Where did you find her? She is adorable."

"She did a face plant in a flowerbed and I am nursing her back to health."

"They say that if you find a pixie, good things will come your way."

Tara picked up a pair of shoes, put them on, then shouted, "Yes! They fit! Can I have them?"

"Sure can. Do you need anything else perhaps? Like dresses, tops, shirts, pants, bed sheets you name it I have it."

"Do you have foundation garments? I am in desperate need of them. Like I don't have any."

"Better yet, let me show you my workshop."

Ralph picked up Tara and followed Emma into a ten by eleven feet room with the walls lined with shelves overflowing with tiny articles. He placed her on a granite table in the center of the room. Emma put two yellow trays full of underwear in front of Tara and said, "Help yourself."

She happily took five of each and thanked her. Emma then loaded Tara down with a complete wardrobe, bedsheets, pillowcases, and blankets. Tara then asked, "Would you mind if I tell my friends about you? Most of them are in rags compared to these clothes."

"I would love it. Would you like some spice tea and scones before you leave?"

Back in the kitchen, Emma served Tara her tea in a handmade wooden mug made for her. Emma poured herself a cup of tea, sat, down and inquired, "Are you still dating that woman Kathleen Summers?"

"No. I'm engaged to her."

Emma sighed, took a swallow of her tea, shook her head, then stated,

"She is no good for you Ralph. That woman is a gold digger and hangs around that loser guy, Frank."

"Kathleen told me that she stopped seeing him."

"All I will say is watch your back when you are around her."

Ralph gave Emma fifty dollars for the clothes she gave Tara, gave her a hug and left."

Back at Ralph's home, Tara flew up to Ralph, gazed in his face saying, "We have to talk. So, you sit on the couch and I'll sit on the end table."

"You up for coffee?"

"Make mine light, no sweetener."

Tara took a swallow of her coffee, looked at Ralph and said, "Kathleen is using you."

Ralph smiled and said, "Do I detect a note of jealousy?"

"No that's not it. Kathleen is after your 1943 copper penny and ring."

"No, you have her all wrong. Kathleen is not that kind of a woman."

"Have you ever wondered why you fall asleep when she gives you a back rub?"

"It helps me relax. No big deal."

Kathleen uses a lotion that has a sedative in it. She then uses that stupid pixie doll to monitor you. Wait here. I want to show you something." Tara came back a minute later, showed Ralph the add from Specialty Laboratories and said, "That woman is after me, and I for one do not want to a probe stuck up my you know what for the rest of my life."

"You are letting your fears of humans get the better of you."

"Listen to me!" shouted Tara, "She had that dip-wad of a Frank in our house running around in your bathrobe, while you were asleep on the floor!"

"I can't believe Kathleen is that kind of a woman. But, I do believe that you are stretching the truth, the way you did with your wings."

"You are impossible!" screamed Tara. "Faigh tríd an cloigeann tiubh de mise le go Kathleen agus scrios amach chugat!" shouted an excited Tara in Irish Gaelic.

"Say What?"

"Sorry. I speak in Irish Gaelic when I get excited, I said, get it through that thick skull of yours that Kathleen is out to destroy you." Tara silently stared at Ralph for a minute then stated, "Can you lean back on the couch?"

"Sure. Now what?"

Tare flew to Ralph's chest to put her arms around his throat for a hug but fell in his lap with one wing twisted wincing in pain.

A puzzled Ralph asked, "Are you trying to con me with a sprained wing?"

Tara stated through clenched teeth, "I've got a wing spasm and I need you to massage my back."

Ralph removed Tara's top, placed her face down between his knee, and gently rubbed her wing muscle until it was back in place. Tara stood, looked down at herself, smiled at Ralph saying in Irish Gaelic, "Ní cúram liom má tá mé, lom, I am going to give you a hug anyway."

"In English, please."

"You'll figure it out, now look out, I'm gonna give you a squeeze."

Ralph felt uncomfortable with Tara giving him a hug when she was bare chested and decided to change the subject and said, "I had a jacuzzi installed in the large shower stall. What do you say we try it out?"

"A What?"

"A Jacuzzi, you know, a big tub with warm churning bubbly water. Wanna try it?"

"Give me a minute to put on my yellow, two-piece bathing suit and I will join you."

Ten minutes later, Tara lie on Ralph's chest in the Jacuzzi and said, "This is the life."

"Tara, can you do me a great big favor? Try being modest for a change. Unless you are trying to tell me something, and I am not listing."

"We are friends and I don't mind you seeing me in my birthday suit. But what bothers me is I don't like it when you are kissing Kathleen, or she is rubbing your back. Because I feel you are mine and she has no business touching you."

"We are friends and we will never be able to marry because I am five feet taller than you."

"I don't mind the difference in our height."

"I mind seeing you in the buff because it is frustrating and wrong." Stated Ralph firmly.

"Like I just said, we are good friends, and I don't mind if you see things."

"Can we change the subject."

Just then the doorbell rang and Kathleen hollered, "Ralph, where are you?"

A panic-stricken Tara stated, "She can't know that I am here." and quickly hid in the narrow space between the wall and the jacuzzi, just as Kathleen walked in and shouted, "Alright a hot tub! I was going to ask you if you wanted to go to the lake for a swim, but this is much better. Make room because I am coming in."

A nervous Ralph stated, "Ah, you don't have a bathing suit on."

"That's not going to stop me."

"I don't think you should be doing this Kathleen." Ralph quickly turned his back as she stepped out of her clothes, then in the Jacuzzi. Kathleen tapped Ralph's shoulder saying, "Relax will ya. I have on a new bikini that I wanted to show you."

Ralph turned back around, eyed Kathleen's dark blue bikini and said, "Nice little thing, but it's on the skimpy side. I have just one question. What do you think the Lord would say about wearing that skimpy bathing suit of yours at the beach?"

Kathleen cuddled up to Ralph and said, "Because you have a strict moral stranded about seeing me in the buff. I bought this bathing suit for your eyes only."

"You didn't answer my question."

Kathleen reached under the churning water, placed her hand on Ralph's hip and asked, "When did you start wearing a skimpy Speedo bathing suit?"

"I figure wearing it in the hot tub would be alright but, I didn't expect you to come over."

"So, there is a playful side of you after all. Stand up so I can take a look at you."

"No, I don't think so."

"Ever since we been dating all I have seen of you is your bare chest and that is only occasion, so stand and let me see what the rest of your body looks like."

"You know that's not true."

"I wanna see so stand up."

Ralph glanced to his right, saw Tara shaking her head no. Then suggested, "Kathleen, what do you say we get dressed and make dinner?" and stood.

Kathleen face broadened into a smile when she saw what little Ralph had on then rubbed his butt. Ralph stated, firmly, "Absolutely not, I know what you want to do next. We get dress before things go any further. You use the bedroom downstairs and I'll use the one upstairs."

"Hey, you can't blame a girl for trying." she then patted his rump again.

Ralph helped Kathleen out of the hot tub, handed her a towel, walked out of the room, closing the door in Tara's face.

Tara picked herself up off the floor hollering, "No, you can't have him! He's mine I tell you. He's all mine!" She then let go a long scream in frustration.

Chapter 6

PINT SIZE RALPH

Later, Kathleen wiped her mouth with her white linen napkin and said, "Ralph, that was the best roast chicken I have ever tasted. I see who is going to do the cooking after we are married."

"Care for dessert? It's Baked Alaska."

"Bring it on?"

Kathleen took a bite of her sweet treat then said, "There are a few things that are bothering me. For one, you see your butter dish. Why is there an imprint of a tiny face in it?"

"My friend came over with his daughter and she dropped her doll in it."

Kathleen took out her tube of red lipstick, handed it to Ralph along with a magnifying glass and asked, "What do you see just below the top?"

"Scratches?"

"Just below that, there is a clear impression of a tiny hand as if a pixie was trying to steal some."

Kathleen showed Ralph a photo and asked, "What do you see?"

"Tiny footprints. Hey, you are good at fabricating this stuff."

"That is a picture of your rug right after we painted. There is a pixie running around this house somewhere and I intend to find it."

Ralph produced the flyer from Specialty Laboratories, and asked, "This fell out of your purse the other day. Are you that heartless that you would sell one of those poor creatures to a Lab and condemning it to a life of misery?"

"I thought you didn't believe in pixies?"

"That flyer makes me think that maybe there are sprites around somewhere."

"That belongs to Frank. He was trying to convince me to go along with his scam."

"So, you faked the hand print in your lipstick and the footprint on the rug to con Frank. However, I have one more question. Why are you still seeing him when you told me you stopped dating him last year? Have you two been in bed together?"

"I would never do anything like that! He may have seen my bare posterior once or twice but that's all. Honest."

"He what?" hollered Ralph on the verge of losing his temper.

"After my shower I ah, went in the kitchen to fix myself something to eat when Frank barges in. I didn't have time to cover myself with a towel as I tried to chase him out but he wouldn't leave until I gave him a hug."

"And, did you?"

"I don't have to report to you what happened between Frank and me in my bedroom yesterday after the hug."

"You were in bed with Frank yesterday?" questioned Ralph, "And you do have to give me a reason why, because we are going to be married. Besides, why are you hanging around him when you supposed to have stopped seeing him last year?"

"Like I told you, Frank is my coffee buddy. No more no less."

"You have coffee with Frank in your bedroom. That is so wrong Kathleen, you can't serve two men. You will either love one and hate the other."

Kathleen reached across the table, held Ralph's hands saying, "I will stop seeing Frank as of right now."

"How many times have you seen Frank's bare," Kathleen stopped Ralph in the middle of his sentence and said. "Let's not go there, okay."

Ralph pulled his hands away from Kathleen's saying, "I see how things are going. Why don't we back away from each other for a while. I cannot marry somebody who is seeing another man."

A shocked Kathleen inquired, "What are you saying? The wedding is off."

"No. not just yet. We need time apart to sort things out, clear the air."

"I'll give you the space you need. But, can I still come over once in a while?"

"I wish you would."

"Bare with me for a minute. Why don't we take a walk hand in hand the way we did when we first met?"

"It's back to the beginning I guess. So let's go."

Back in his house shortly after one in the morning, Ralph gave Kathleen a halfhearted kiss and said, "I'll be seeing you." With his head spinning with thoughts of his Sweetheart in bed with Frank. He went upstairs, washed up and crawled in bed.

The next morning Ralph fixed his breakfast, sat down to eat, paused and thought, "*Something isn't right.*" he then shouted, "Tara! Where is she?"

He heard a faint banging and went to investigate. Upon opening the door to the hot tub room. There stood Tare looking up at him with her arms folded across her chest. She grumbled, "It's about time you let me out. Did you have a fun time cheating on me?"

"I don't have the time for your foolishness this morning Tara, come to breakfast."

"You had plenty of time for her yesterday. What about me? When did she leave, this morning?"

"Back off, you little Imp!" roared Ralph, "If you want food, get it yourself! I'm out of here!"

Tara's mouth dropped open, stunned at Ralph's reactions. She then thought, "*There is trouble between Kathleen and Ralph. Now that I got what I wanted, I feel like crap.*"

Forty minutes later, Tara found Ralph brooding on the back deck. She kicked and banged on the sliding glass door to get Ralph to open it but he paid no attention to her. Tara frantically searched the house until she found the open flue in the fireplace. Soared up and out the chimney, then down, landing on Ralph's right shoulder saying, "A nickel for your thoughts?"

"I want to be left alone." and brushed her off his shoulder.

Tara squealed as she lost her balance, and tumbled to the deck. Ralph quickly picked her up and apologized.

Tara smiled, and said, "You need a hug."

Gary T. Brideau

"You better get inside before someone sees you. Oh, you look great in that bathing suit. It shows off your nice figure."

Inside, Tara asked, "Can you take off your shirt? I want to give you a back rub."

In the bedroom on the first floor, Ralph lay on the bed without his shirt. Tara climbed on top of him, squeezed some lotion on him and proceed to massage his back. Only to wind up slipping and sliding on the lotion.

Twenty minutes later, Tara lay prostrate on Ralph's back panting and said, "I give up. Giving a human, a back rub is one tough job."

"You did pretty good, for someone your size."

"You think so?"

"I know so."

"I have an idea. Why don't you brew up a pot of Cinnamon Tea, bring it downstairs to my place? Then you can soak your feet in the pond while we drink our tea. After, we can play on the mountain water slide."

"Don't you mean you?"

"Yeah, I ah got carried away."

In the basement, Ralph filled Tara's mug with tea, then he, took off his shoes and socks, rolled up his pant legs and stuck his feet in the slow-moving water.

While Ralph was doing that, Tare sprinkled some green herb in his hot drink. Ralph took a swallow, held his head saying, "Whoa, I feel dizzy all of a sudden." He dropped his mug, fell back on the grass, and passed out.

A minute later, a tiny Ralph poked his head out of the left leg of his pants, glanced around and bellowed, "Tara! What did you do to me?"

Tara approached Ralph, gazed at him, giggled and handed him a pair of yellow bathing trunks saying, "You'll need these. Unless you like skinny-dipping."

Ralph put on his bathing suit then demanded, "Make me big again, right now!"

"Can't, the shrinking powder has to wear off. When that happens, you will sneeze three times, then you will return to your normal size. Which will be about twenty-four hours from now. Until then, let's have fun." Tara stared at Ralph's fallen countenance, hung her head saying, "I was hoping by you being my size it would cheer you up."

Ralph scanned the vast basement, smiled, took Tara in his arms, and gave her a passionate kiss on her lips. Looked her in her eyes and said, "You don't know how long I wanted to do that. But, first, you have to show me you home.

Three hours later, Ralph walked out of Tara's home with a radiant smile on his face. Stopped, gave her another kiss then stated, "Kathleen never gave me a back rub like that."

"What do you say we have fun on the mountain water slide?"

"That's just what I was thinking of."

Two hours later, Tara and Ralph sat snuggled together on the bank by the pond. Ralph stated, "I never knew being with a woman could be so much fun. It's like I have been asleep all my life."

"No, just in a stupor that's all. What did you do with Kathleen? If you don't mind me asking?"

"We went to operas where a woman's singing sounded like someone was torturing a cat. We went to classical music concerts that put me to sleep. We'd go to the lake, occasionally, but we never went in the water. Oh yes, there were Kathleen's dinner parties where everyone was dressed in tuxedos." Tare stared at Ralph and asked, "And you want to marry this woman? Is there anything that bothers you about her?"

"Yes. She likes to have coffee with her male friend, Frank. Which I am totally against. That's why I was upset today. And I am sorry if I hurt you."

Tara motioned Ralph to be still, she then counted the chimes on the grandfather's clock upstairs in the living room, then said, "Wow! It's six in the morning. We have been up all night."

"It only seemed like a few hours to me."

"Hey, you wanna explore the caves in the mountain? They are so cool."

"Why not. After all, I built them."

Two hours later, back on the bank, Tara tossed some pillows and blanket on the grass saying, "I'm bushed. I think it's safer if we sleep out here instead of in my bed."

Ralph spread the blankets on the grass, put the pillows and blankets in place then snuggled up to Tara under them.

Five that afternoon Ralph woke with Tara lying on her side looking at him with a smile on her face. He inquired, "Is there something wrong?"

"No. I just like watching you sleep that's all."

"I wish I could make us something to eat, but being this small I am helpless."

"I got you covered. I'll fly up to the kitchen and get us something."

"Be careful that you don't have a wing cramp."

Tara kissed Ralph, soared up the clothes shut and opened the panel trying to figure out what she was going to get for them to eat.

Sanding on the eating counter Tara stared at the fridge when a twelve-pound orange cat jumped up with her. Tara hollered, "Whoa! Where did you come from?" then flew to the dining room table with the cat trying to catch her.

Sitting on the chandelier over the dining room table, Tara studied the cat's movements. Then tried to make it back to the laundry shoot but the cat was too fast and almost caught her. Back on the chandelier Tare spotted the sliding glass door ajar and muttered, "So that's how Mr. Kitty got in. But, how do I get him back out? If I can access a dog barking on Ralph's computer that should scare Mr. Kitty."

Tara soared around the kitchen, hopped from picture to curtain rod hoping to confuse the cat before flying down the hall and into the den.

In the den, she had only typed the second letter when the cat jumped on the keyboard. Tara leaped in the air, then dropped in the small space between the wall and the desk. The cat's paw brushed Tara's shoulder several times as it tried to reach her.

She spotted a laser pointer on the floor three feet from her. Tara made a dash for it, turned it on. The cat forgot about Tara and began to play with the spot of light. With the pointer in her hand, Tara kept the light in front of the cat as it chased the small point of light to the open sliding glass door. Tara stated, "Dang! It's too bright outside for the pointer to work. She took a deep breath, and muttered,

"Here goes nothing." flew down and rammed the cat's hind end as hard as she could with her head. The cat squealed as it darted out the door and off the back deck.

With the sliding glass door closed, Tare went about trying to find something to eat.

Back in the basement, Tara put down a hot dog wrapped in a napkin saying, "I hope this will do for now."

"That's more than enough, Thank you." Ralph then questioned, "Why do you smell like poop?"

"I had to take care of Mr. Kitty first and had to boot him out with my head."

"Come here." Ralph held a trembling Tara in his arms, she put her head on his shoulder, and cried, "A couple of times I thought I was going to be a kitty snack."

"Tara, you are ripe. I think you should wash your hair first, then we can eat."

After, Ralph scanned his surrounding, and stated, "I think I'll remove those pixie dolls. I never knew how creepy they look from your angle." Ralph turned Tara around, touched Tara's back saying, "You need another back rub. I don't like the looks of your wings."

"My wings feel fine. You just want an excuse to touch me that's all."

"Guilty as charged."

Tara lay face down on the blanket, ready for her back rub, but nothing happened.

She rolled on her back, looked up at Ralph and inquired, "Is there something wrong?"

"Yes plenty. I want to do more than a back rub. I want to hum."

Tara stood, placed her finger on his lips saying, "I would be blessed to mate with you. But, not right now because the Bible says it's wrong."

"You have been reading the Word."

"Yes. Would it be too much to ask if we could snuggle before you return to your normal size?"

Chapter 7

RALPH TO THE RESCUE

Shortly after 12 AM Ralph returned to his normal size, went upstairs, picked up his Bible, sat in his gray recliner and read the Word of God. He then asked," Lord, Kathleen is a wonderful woman and we see eye to eye on so many things. True, we have a few problems, but we can work it out with Your guidance. But what bothers me is Tara. She excites me in ways that I never thought possible. She makes me feel masculine and that I am the important one in her life. She is more of a woman than Kathleen ever could be. I wouldn't have a problem with her, but she is a pixie, a one-foot tall Pixie."

The thought entered Ralph's mind, *"She is still a woman who needs your help."*

"True Lord, if you hide her wings she is just a small human being. Be that as it may, it's going to be difficult dating a woman that tiny. Oh, a Lord. Tara told me that Kathleen is two faced and is trying to con me out of my money. I'm not sure whether to believe her or not. It could be that Tara's jealousy is speaking. I am not sure.

Oh, one more thing Lord. Thank you for your forgiveness when I fooled around with Tara when we were under the blanket. Please help me not to mess up that way again. Amen."

Early the next morning in the master bedroom, Tara lifted Ralph's right eyelid saying, "Wakey, wakey. It's way past breakfast time."

Ralph stared at Tara and said, "I like your Robin Hood outfit and crossbow. Now, do me a favor? Turn on the air conditioner to high cool, then turn on the shower for me."

Half asleep. Ralph closed the shower door, and let the warm water cascade down his sore body, glanced at the door, and said, "Tara what are you doing sitting on top of the shower door watching me?"

"I was wondering why are you showering in your Pjs? I forgot to tell you. The side effect of being shrunk is, extreme fatigue."

"That explains a lot."

"Can I help you in some way?"

"Yes. Help me take off my Pjs."

After a shower and a healthy meal, Ralph collapsed in the recliner in a fresh pair of pajamas bottoms and fell asleep.

Kathleen entered the house a short time later, saw Ralph resting, slipped him a sedative then motioned for Frank to join her. She then stated, "No walking around in Ralph's robe and slippers this time, we have work to do."

"What about him?"

"He's out for at least five hours. Now, get searching!"

"Not before I make myself something to eat."

"If Ralph finds out that we've been here, you are gonna hear it from Stan not me, so get moving. There are three more bedrooms, the den, the attic and the basement left to search!"

Tara slowly parted the Boston Fern, raised her crossbow then shot a sewing needle in Franks' thigh. He hollered, turned around and shouted, "What's the big idea sticking me with a needle? I'm gonna look but first I'm gonna make myself a sandwich and have a can of coke."

"What are you talking about? I didn't stab you."

Tara giggled, then let another needle fly that struck Franks back left shoulder. He pulled it out, spun around swiftly and shouted, "That's enough Kathleen! You stick me one more time and you can find that penny yourself!"

"How could I stick you from the opposite side of the room? Stop trying to start an argument and find the penny."

Tara then shot Ralph in his left shoulder to wake him. He brushed the needle out and groaned, "Who's here?"

Kathleen quickly ripped off her dress, and underwear, then motioned for Frank to grab her. He pushed her to the floor as Kathleen whispered, "Open your pants, and make like you are trying to assault me."

Through blurry eyes, Ralph saw, Kathleen crying for help as she struggled with Frank on top of her. He sprang out of the recliner, grabbed Frank by his shirt collar, hauled him off Kathleen, then landed a right cross to his jaw. Kathleen fell into Ralph's arms sobbing, as Frank ran out the door.

A grateful Kathleen smothered Ralph with kisses and she pulled him down on the floor. Ralph stopped Kathleen and said, "Please put your clothes on."

"Why? I am thankful that you woke in time to stop that brute of a Frank, I don't care that I am not dressed. Now, show me how much you love me." and pulled down Ralph's Pj bottoms. He turned, spotted Tara watching from the fern, broke away from his girlfriend, made himself decent, then looked at Kathleen, and said, "Pleases, put your clothes back on."

Kathleen held Ralph in her arms and asked, "Why?"

"Just do it, okay."

Later, sitting at the dining room table, Kathleen had on Ralph's robe as he served coffee her coffee, took a swallow of his and asked, "What were you doing in my house with Frank?"

Kathleen tried to look innocent as she stated, "I called Frank and told him that I wanted to meet him at the Burger Joint and that I had to talk to him. When I told him that we were through, he became violent and threatened to kill me. I didn't know where to go for help so I came here hoping to get away from him. But, he barges in and tried to rape me. That's when you woke."

A concerned Ralph asked, "Do you think you will be able to drive home tonight?"

"Could I stay here for the night? I'm pretty shaken up. As you can see Frank tore my clothes all to pieces, and my booby-catcher isn't in the best shape either. I'd use one of your shirts but none of them will fit me if you know what I mean. So, I guess I am gonna have to walk around like this until I can find something to put on."

Ralph stared at his girlfriend and stated, "I don't care how you are dressed, I have a lot of work to do downstairs which means I won't be seeing you for most the night."

In the basement, Ralph pulled up the legs of his Pjs, put his feet in the pond and stared at the mountain trying to figure out how he could improve it. Tara lit on Ralph's right shoulder, and said, "Nickel for your thoughts."

"Hi, Little Sweetheart. Better not talk too loud, Kathleen will hear you."

Tara whispered, "Do you want to hear my version of what happened?"

"Okay, Shoot."

Kathleen and Frank were here hoping to find your penny. But, I shot Frank with my trusty crossbow to stop him. Then, I shot you to wake you. Kathleen tore her clothes off and had Frank play along with her."

"So, Frank wasn't trying to force himself on her."

"That's right. Kathleen was played the damsel in distress, and you danced pretty good as a puppet."

Tara put her arm around Ralph's neck, leaned against his head and asked, "Why did you stop? I mean Kathleen was ready and waiting for you, all you had to do was assume the lover's position and go for it."

"It felt empty and shallow, compared to what we shared last night. Besides the Lord fronds on that sort of thing."

A surprised Tara asked, "You actually enjoyed doing what we did together?"

"I did things with you that I never did with any woman."

"Whoa, that says a lot, and I am sorry for touching your butt when I gave you that back rub."

"You may be twelve inches tall, but there is a lot more woman inside of you than in Kathleen." A puzzled Ralph glanced at Tara and said, "When I was on the rug with Kathleen, you were getting ready to shoot me in the butt with a needle."

"No. I was ready to ram it in your bottom as hard as I could. If you continued with her."

Ralph then asked, "What do you use the garage for?"

"What's a garage?"

"The place where you put cars and junk."

"Oh, the room with the flip up wall. That's my Laboratory, where

I keep my spices, herbs things so I can use them on people. The green powdered moss mixed with just the right spices, put in Cinnamon tea, will shrink a human."

"That's witchcraft."

"Bite your tongue for saying that. I am a Pixie who deals in drugs, sort of speak. I know what herb to use, to cause the right reactions in people. Like a pinch of dark blue powder in the catalyst, Earl Gray tea will cause memory loss. Or white crystals blow in someone's face, will put them to sleep. No Hocus-Pocus, it's just knowing the right herbs to put in the right catalyst. which is various kinds of tea or coffee. If I put the green moss powder in Earl-Gray it would only enhance the flavor."

"Is there an herb for lovers?"

"You better believe there is. But I won't use it." Tara looked up then said, "I want to check on your girlfriend," Tara zipped in her lab, sprinkled just the right herbs in her hand, flew up the dirty clothes shoot, found Kathleen in the den going through Ralph's desk, shouted, "Hey Bug Nuggets! Over here!"

"A pixie! I knew it." shouted Kathleen, she then asked sweetly, "Would you like to come home with me?"

"For what? So, you can sell me to a lab? No thank you."

As soon as Kathleen was a foot from her, Tara opened her hand and blew the powder in her face. Kathleen's eyes rolled back in her head as she collapsed on the floor, sound asleep.

Tara pointed her finger at Kathleen saying, "That's what you get for messing with my man."

Back in the basement, Ralph inquired, "I heard a thump. What happened?"

Tara snickered, "I put Miss Busybody to sleep."

Ralph stared at Tara and asked, "And what else?"

"I used just enough sleeping crystals with a little 'Forget Me Not,' powder to put her to sleep and forget that she saw me."

"And what else?"

"Nothing, honest I just put her to sleep to forget me, and a dash of Fire Mushroom so she will have red welts all over her in the morning."

"Annnd?"

"Alright, she is going to have red welt with a wrapper of a headache."

48

"Tara, what am I going to do with you?"

"Love me. Hey, a pixie has to fight for what is hers and I am not going to let that She-devil have you. Now lie on your back so I can help you relax. Fire Mushrooms powdered mixed with the right spices is a great remedy to warm your skin." Tara then blew a pink dust that settled on Ralph's back, he smiled saying, "That feels soooo good."

Tara smiled saying, "And he's out."

Tara sat on the mountain overlooking the pond, and cried, "Mom. I wish you were here so you can tell me if I am doing the right thing by staying with this human."

The name Emma flashed in Tara's mind. She left a note, squeezed out the mail slot and flew to Emma's house. She squeezed in her mail slot and found Emma busy making tiny shoes. Tara sat on the work table, and inquired, "I need someone to talk to."

Emma served tea and scones, sat at the kitchen table, and asked, "What's on your mind?"

"I like Ralph allot, but he loves Kathleen and it feels like I am doing wrong by getting in the middle of them. If by some small chance Ralph sides with me, how am I going to take care of my man who is five feet taller than me? I can't give him a son, go food shopping or any of the things a wife does. So, if you could give me a backpack, that I can put a few things in, I'll be on my way."

"If that's what you think you should do. I'll get a backpack. But, what will happen to Ralph when you leave him in her hands?"

"Ralph would miss me, marry Kathleen who would take all his money, then leave him for Frank. Which would put Ralph on the street knowing Kathleen. But, what can I do? I'm just a pixie."

"If that's what you believe, then that's all you will be, just a pixie. Remember, it's not the size of the pixie, it's the size of the heart that is in the pixie that matters."

Tara smiled and said, "Ralph told me that I was more of a woman than Kathleen. Not that Ralph and I got into things."

"You would have to use the powdered green moss so shrink him to do that."

Tara stared at Emma wondering how she knew what she did with Ralph that night, then said, "I must be on my way."

"Why don't you stay here tonight, there are too many night creature out there who will make a delicious meal of you."

"Could I have another cup of tea, please?"

"Would you like a doughnut with that too?"

"Oh boy would I."

Tara woke the next morning in a canopy bed in Emma's workshop. Looked up at her and said, "Thanks for the bunny Pjs, it sure beats what I've been wearing. What can I do to pay you for them?"

"You already have by telling your little friends about me."

"They contacted you already?"

"I even have some of them working for me in order to keep up with the orders. My best worker is Corina, boy can that pixie work."

"Gotta get back to my man, and thanks, Emma."

"Oh, I have to tell you that I put some black powder in your knapsack. Use it sparingly. A little sniff will last six hours."

Chapter 8

TARA, BIG AND TALL

On her way back home, Tara flew high enough so the people on the ground wouldn't recognize her as a pixie. She glanced up and saw a hawk diving for her. Tara folded her arms, and plummeted like a bullet, then suddenly flew left, just as the hawk soared by her. Tara then flew from tree to tree with one eye on the sky praying that the bird would not make a return visit.

At home, Tara flew down the chimney, and out the hearth, landed on the fern and stared at Ralph in his Pjs bottoms and Kathleen in a bathrobe, lying to gather on the couch kissing. Tara grabbed a match, flew down the hall, lit it, then blew out, setting off the smoke detector.

Ralph rushed to turn it off, saw Tara hovering just below it with her arms folded across her chest. He smiled sheepishly, and said, "I can explain."

Tara whispered, "I want her out of our house, now!"

"She doesn't have any clothes to put on."

"Throw her out in her birthday suit, I don't care. Just get rid of that Trollop."

Kathleen walked up to Ralph with her robe partly open and asked, "Who are you talking to Hon?"

Ralph quickly stuffed the pixie down inside his Pjs bottoms and said, "No one, just muttering to myself about this dumb smoke detector."

Kathleen put her arms around Ralph's neck saying, "Come back to the couch so we can continue." and rubbed Ralph's back before she left.

Tara dug her fingernails into Ralph's inner thigh and whispered, "Don't even think of it, Mister."

"You will have to Trust me."

Tara whispered from inside Ralph's Pjs, "If she isn't out of here in five minutes, you will have to deal with me, and trust me you do not want to get me angry."

"But she doesn't have anything to wear."

"What about that big red plaid shirt your mother gave you? It should fit Miss Sarah Bernhardt."

Ralph put Tara in the laundry shut saying, "We'll talk later." approached Kathleen and said, "Now that your headache is gone, let's see if we can find you something to put on." then he closed her robe.

"What about the red blotches all over me? I can't drive home sick."

Ralph handed Kathleen a shirt and a pair his jeans, then told her to dress in the bathroom.

Later, a dressed, Kathleen glared at Ralph and said, "I don't understand. One minute we are making out on the couch, the next you are rushing me out the door. Why the bum's rush? Or should I be asking, "Who is she?"

Ralph smiled and said, "I told you I have been seeing a pixie by the name of Tara, and she is the cutest little thing I've ever seen. But when it comes to being kittenish, that pixie knows how to have fun."

"You are not being cute, Ralph, just obnoxious."

"Talk to you later Sweet and be careful on the way home."

Ralph put on his black pants, a blue shirt, black shoes and went downstairs. Knocked on Tara's front door and asked, "Are you in there?"

"Go away, I don't want to talk to you."

"Where did you go last night? I missed you lifting my eyelid this morning."

Tara opened the front door and said, "If you must know, I was thinking of moving on because you don't need me. Emma told me to stay but when I saw you in Kathleen's arms, I wonder if what you told me earlier was true. Or were you telling me that to stroke my ego?"

"You have every right to be mad at me for the way I acted around Kathleen. But you must understand that I have been dating her for over two years, and planned to marry her soon."

Tara stated, "Then you met me and I turned your entire world upside-down. Part of you wants to throw caution to the wind and enjoy the fantastic time with me. Then there is the other side of you that wants to be prudish and decent, so Kathleen can clean you out of all your money."

Ralph stared at Tara and asked, "What happened on your way home?"

Tara sat on Ralph's right shoulder, and said, "I was almost hawk food."

Ralph folded his arms across his chest, Tara stood on his arms, grabbed his shirt, and cried.

Later, he found a tree in the basement, sat down, and leaned back, put Tara in his lap and asked, "Tell me about your home life."

"There was just me and my mom and dad. Mom always had a word of wisdom for me to live by and dad taught me the drug business. One morning I put on my favorite red dress, dad told me to pick some fire mushrooms. But when I got back, my home it was demolished and there was no sight of mom and dad. That's when a bird grabbed me by the back of my dress. I ripped it off and I barely escaped being the bird's lunch."

"So, the rags you had on was what was left of your dress."

"You guessed it. That was the same day I slammed into you in the garden trying to get away from that bird the second time."

"So, you hold onto me out of fear that you are gonna lose me too."

Tara suddenly perked up, hid behind Ralph just as Kathleen approached him and asked, "Where is she?"

"Where is who?"

"The pixie you have been living with. That's who."

"Have you been drinking Kathleen? Because that sounds like something that would come out of a liquor bottle."

"You told me twice that you were dating a pixie. Now, where is she?"

"You were looking for a woman, so I made up a sprite."

"She is hiding behind you." Kathleen pushed Ralph on his side, just as Tara scurried in the bushes, then up his pant leg when he stood. Tara then held onto Ralph's underwear as he asked his girlfriend, "Are you finished tearing my inside garden apart?"

"I will find that pixie no matter how long it takes me."

Ralph held Kathleen's shoulders and asked, "What has gotten into you here of lately? This is not the woman I fell in love with. She was sweet, kind and giving. Why this obsession with money?"

"You wouldn't understand even if I told you."

"You will have to see yourself out because I have a slight cramp in my leg. Oh, one more thing, Please, please ring the doorbell before you come in. I do not want you walking in on me unannounced."

With Kathleen gone, Tara fell out of Ralph's pant leg on the grass coughing and gagging.

Ralph inquired, "Are you alright?"

"No, I'm not. Did you have to cut the cheese when I was hiding inside your pant leg?"

"Sorry, I have a nervous stomach."

"You need something to clean you out because that was rank."

"Back to what we were talking about. I am so sorry that you lost your parents."

"I didn't see any blood or body parts, so they may be still alive." Could you please give me a back rub? My wings muscles are not used to that much flying.

A brief time later, Tara lay on the grass in her white bikini. Ralph lie next to her rubbing his index finger up and down her back.

Tara muttered, "This feels so good. You have just the right touch."

Kathleen quietly approached and said, "How interesting. My husband to be getting kinky with a pixie."

"Kathleen!" shouted Ralph in surprise. "What are you doing here?"

"You lied to me!"

"I told you that I was seeing a pixie by the name of Tara. But she didn't want to meet you and you lied to me when you told me that you were going home."

"Did you really think that I was going to walk away when I knew there was a pixie around?"

Tara stood, glared up at Kathleen and asked, "Are you going to tell Ralph that you've been cheating on him with Frank, or should I? Better yet, why don't you tell your husband to be that you put him to sleep with a sedative in that lotion so you and Frank can steal his 1943 penny?"

Kathleen tried to scoop up the pixie with her hand but Tara jumped in the bushes nearby, saying, "You humans are so clumsy."

"Now, I have you." stated Kathleen as she picked up Tara in her right hand.

Tara hollered, "Let me go you Trollop!" she then sunk her teeth in Kathleen's finger. Kathleen screamed, then threw the pixie. Tara hollered, "Boomerang flight!" and landed feet first into Kathleen's nose causing it to bleed.

Tara picked up her knapsack, took a pinch of black powder in her hand, and said, "No more miss nice pixie. Lady, I'm taking you down."

"Yeah. A foot-high imp is gonna kick my butt. I don't think so."

With her eyes on Kathleen, Tara put her hand to her face inhaled the powder. Let out a screech, and shot up to six feet tall. Picked up Kathleen by her throat saying, "I think so." then landed a blow to her stomach with her left hand, then dropped her.

A stunned Kathleen stared at Tara with her eyes blazing and her wings buzzing, and asked, "H, how did you do that?"

"You think you're gonna sell me to a lab for money? Not in my lifetime lady."

Kathleen locked her gaze on Ralph and said, "Do something before that thing kills me."

"Tara is not a thing. she's a human with her wings. If you flatten her wings against her back there is no difference between the two of you, and from where I am standing Tara is more of a human than you are."

"How can't say that when we are going to be married."

"How can you say that you love me when you've been in bed with Frank on a regular bases."

"I have never cheated on you, Ralph. That thing has been putting thoughts in your mind."

Tara spoke up saying, "Kathleen, do you want me to tell Ralph about the rubdown you gave Frank after you took a shower with him?"

"I don't have to stand here and be insulted like this," stated Kathleen. "I might as well tell you, Patsy next door dropped off a garbage bag full of clothes hoping you knew what to do with them."

Tara grabbed Kathleen's by the back of her blouse and the seat the seat of her pants and ushered her upstairs to the front door then said, "Don't come back."

Two minutes later, Ralph stared at Tara in standing in the middle of the living room in her altogether and said, "You look great like that, but, if I know Kathleen she is gonna go right to the police so you need to put some clothes on to hide your wings."

Out of curiosity, Tara opened the garbage bag that Patsy left, found a paisley dress that fit her and put it on with her wings underneath.

Ralph stared at Tara and said, "That dress makes you look gorgeous. I'll make some coffee then we will sit and talk."

While Ralph and Tara were talking in the living room, the front doorbell rang. Tara answered the door saying, "Officers, come in. Can I get you a cup of coffee?"

One officer stated, "I had a report of a domestic violence."

Ralph answered, "My girlfriend Kathleen was here and did not like the idea of me entertaining this fine lady and she got a little testy, so I asked her to leave."

"Are you engaged to Miss Summers?"

"Yes, I am but things are not working out for us so I told her that I needed some space. But she keeps entering my home unannounced."

"My advice to you is to change the locks on the door."

After the police had left, Ralph asked Tara, "How?"

"Emma gave me some black powder just in case I needed it. Oh, Black powder makes a pixie grow, but we are to use it in case of dire emergency. Before we were interrupted, you were massaging my back."

Ralph reached in the garbage bag, handed Tara a canary yellow, one-piece bathing suit and said, "Put this on first."

After Ralph gave Tara a long back rub, she dressed and said, 'I have four hours left before I shrink back to my normal size. I want to see how the humans live."

Ralph stared at Tara wiggling her toes and said, "We have to get you some shoes. Because there isn't a restaurant around that will let you in without shoes on."

Sometime later, Ralph was leaving the shoe store with Tara and bumped into his parents. His mother gave him a hug saying, "How's my boy doing?" She glanced at Tart and inquired, "Where is that nice girl Kathleen?"

"We are having difficulty and are not seeing each other. Oh. mom this is Tara Jones. Gotta go."

Ralph's father shook his son's hand saying, "Dump the other one. This one's a keeper."

Just as they reached the car, Ralph's pastor walked up to him and asked, "Is everything alright with you and Kathleen? Because the wedding is in three weeks."

"We stopped seeing each other for a while because of problems."

"Dating someone else is not the way to heal a relationship."

"Pastor, this Tara Jones a friend of mine."

"I must say, ma'am, that there is a radiance about you that is remarkable."

Tara smiled and said, "I've been reading about a man in a book and he seems very extraordinary, loving and kind. You look like an intelligent man that I can ask you this question. How can I meet Jesus?"

"You do know that Christ died on the Cross to provide salvation, Healing, and Deliverance for Mankind's needs. What you need to do right now is acknowledge that you are a sinner, separated from God, believe that Christ rose from the dead, and confess your sins to Him and receive Him into your heart as Lord and Savior. Then find a good church."

"Does that include me too?"

"The Word of God says whosoever will, may come if you are a whoever you welcome at the cross."

After Tara gave her life to Christ, the pastor stared at her and said to Ralph "This may sound strange, but I'm going to put the wedding on hold and don't let this woman out of your sight."

Ralph stared at the pastor then said, "For a long time you've been telling me that Kathleen is the one for me and that she is the woman that I should have by my side."

"I am sorry I was wrong. Talk to you later Lord Bless you two."

Chapter 9

A TIME TO PROTECT

In Ralph's car, Tara took off her shoes asked, "How can you humans wear these contraptions? They hurt my feet and what is this fancy bag with a snap on it?"

"It is called a purse. Women put all kinds of things in and shoes are something you have to get used to."

"The shoes Emma made were comfortable, but I guess it all depends on who makes them."

Ralph glanced at Tara out of the corner of his eye in wonderment but stayed silent. He stopped in front of a high classed restaurant. The parking valet parked the car as they entered.

Inside, the maitre-d stared at Tara's bare feet, then in her smiling eyes. Bowed slightly saying, "Barefoot Princess, it is indeed a pleasure to have you here. Where would my lady like to sit?"

"By that row of flowers would be nice."

Seated at the table, Ralph inquired, "What is going on Tara? Everyone we meet treats you like royalty. The woman in the shoe store kept bowing and fell over backward trying to get you the shoes and socks you liked."

Tara smiled and asked, "Can we order? I am starved." She glanced at the yellow flowers growing in a long flower pot to her right and saw something move. She then ordered, "I'll have the Tilapia mashed potshots, and corn with a garden salad."

Ralph ordered the same and asked for tea for the both of them. He then stared at Tara wondering what secret she was hiding.

Without anyone seeing her, Tara slowly parted the flowers, saw a pixie trying to hide. She smiled at her, opened her purse, and placed it in the flowerbed. When the pixie crawled in Tara's purse she picked it up and carefully closed it. When they served the warm rolls, Tara broke off a chunk, put in her purse, smiled sheepishly saying, "It's for later."

In the car after the dinner, Ralph stared at Tara and said, "You may not know this but a woman's purse is not storage for food."

Tara opened her purse, a well-dressed Pixie poked her head out and said, "Hi."

Tara stated, "Ralph, I would like you to meet, Corina. I rescued her from the restaurant this evening."

"What was she doing in there, to begin with?"

Corina spoke up, "Hey. Human, I'm down here. You have something to say about me. talk to me, not over my head like I'm not here."

"Sorry."

"You better be."

"Be nice, Corina." stated Tara, "Now, what were you doing in there when you know human establishments are off limits."

"I was on my way to order some supplies when this heavenly aroma entered my nostrils. So, I just had to investigate the matter."

"Corina. How you can eat so much and yet stay thin is beyond me," stated Tara.

"Is Emma's phone out of order?" asked Ralph.

"Oh yeah, big time."

"Let's get you back to Emma's where you will be safe."

At Emma's, Corina asked her, "Do you have something I can nosh on? I'm a little peckish."

Emma gave Corina a cup of tea and a scone, stared at Tara and said, "How are you holding up?"

"Pretty good concerning the fact that I've been almost eaten by a bird three times, almost killed by a human and had nightmares, however, if it wasn't for my man Ralph who kept me going, I don't know what I would have done."

Emma locked her gaze on Ralph and said, "You have to keep a constant watch on Tara. Her life depends on you to protect her."

"Do you want to tell me what's going on and why people are calling her 'The Barefoot Princess?'"

"It is a form of respect. However, someone is out to kill Tara and steal her drugs."

"Do you know whom?"

"All the sprites know, is that the person will stop at nothing to accomplish the grim task."

"Could that be the reason why my sweet Kathleen turned to evil?"

"She was probably compromised." Emma placed a backpack on the table saying, "The Pixies designed this for Tara, it is made from leather, reinforced with light aluminum so it can't be crushed. Inside is a comfortable seat, a light, a fan hooked up to an air vent to keep the pack cool. Plus, earphones so she can listen to music and last a rack that holds tubes of water."

"It's like a little house. That's cool."

"Oh, I almost forgot. Under the seat is a compartment to store clothes." Emma looked at Tara and said, "There is no word about your mom and dad yet. But don't give up hope."

Emma hollerede, "It's time to come out now!"

Four Pixies dressed all in green each with a crossbow landed on the kitchen table. Emma stated, "I would like you to meet; Misty, Ditsy, Missy, and Mitty. These four will protect Tara and your home from all invasions."

Ralph stared at the Pixie's and said, "They don't look like they can be of much help."

"Looks aren't everything. Observe." Within a minute Ralph was on the floor hogtied. He smiled up at the four and said, "Okay, you convinced me. But how am I going to transport four Pixies to my house?"

"They will find their way there."

Ralph stared at the four and said, "You guys will live in the basement and stay out of my hot tub."

Misty's eyes lit up as she asked, "You have a hot tub?"

"Yes, and it's off limits."

Tara stated, "He also has a mountain water slide and a pond."

Ditsy groaned, "Do we have to stay in your basement? What's the matter? Are you ashamed of being seen with pixies?"

"No. My girlfriend would love to sell you to a lab, where they will stick a probe up your little you know what."

Ditsy quickly straightened up, put her hand on her butt saying, "The basement sounds fine."

Mitty inquired, "Are there any big spiders in your basement that will sink their fangs into my little body?"

"Oh yeah. There is this big black hairy spider that likes to sneak up on you at night. Then wait for you to open your eyes so he can hear you scream as he sinks his fangs into your stomach. Then, when you immobilized by its poison, and unable to scream he will suck every ounce of fluid from your body."

"Mommy." cried a terrified Mitty.

Tara hit Ralph on his shoulder saying, "Will you stop scaring poor little Mitty." she picked up the frightened Pixie and said, "Don't listen to Ralph. There are no spiders in his basement, and we better go home before I return to my normal size."

Home, Ralph showed the four new pixie's his basement and questioned, "What do you think of it ladies?"

Missy, the leader of the group stated, "We'll bivouac outside, Mitty set up a camp fire, the rest of you girls set up your tents." Missy looked up at Ralph and ordered, "It's time you vacated the area. Now that Tara is back to normal, we are gonna go swimming without our bathing suits."

Tara hollered, "Last one in cooks dinner!"

Mitty spread out a towel to lay down saying, "I do not like walking around without anything on So, I'm gonna lay here and snooze."

A Goliath spider, some 12 inches in length slowly crept its way to the unsuspecting pixie resting on her towel.

Ditsy spotted the huge spider approaching her friend and hollered, "Mitty, get out of there! A spider is behind you!"

"Can it will ya guys. Tara said that there are no spiders in this basement."

Mitty rolled on her back saw the spider inches from her feet and froze in fear, Tara took flight, scooped her friend in her arms then landed on the mountain. Mitty stared at the arachnid saying, "Th, that's a huge spider."

"We are safe here because it can't swim."

Missy asked, "We can't stay here until Ralph comes back from shopping. So, what are we going to do? We can't kill the thing because our weapons are over there where it is."

Ditsy pointed to the spider on the wall and said, "Guess who wants to join us?"

Missy stated, "Ditsy, you get in the cave where it can't reach you. The rest of us will go for our bows."

"Thanks a lot, guys, I get to be spider food, while you four fly to safety. I'll remember this when Christmas comes."

With the spider trying to reach Ditsy hunkered in the cave. The Pixie Archers quickly fashioned fire arrows and shot them at the spider. It reared back in flames, lost its grip, and tumbled down the mountain and into the water, dead.

Missy ordered, "Get dressed and arm yourselves, then search every inch of this basement for more of them. Tara, you stay with me."

Tara stared at the dead spider floating in the water and asked, "Are you sure that it is dead?"

Missy shot an arrow through the spider's head and said, "If it wasn't it, is now."

Missy turned to Tara and inquired, "How big is this basement?"

"The woods take up three-quarters of it."

Missy wondered, "What's keeping my girls they should be back by now."

Kathleen walked up to Tara and Missy, with the three missing pixies in the glass jar. stood at the edge of the pond and said, "I see you took care of my pet. Tara, you are coming with me or your friends go for their last swim."

"Don't go with her Tara." stated Missy.

"What do you want to do with me?"

"You are gonna make me rich."

Missy aimed her crossbow at Kathleen saying, "Put down my girls or I'll drop you right where you stand."

Kathleen stared at Missy and laughed, "You have got to be kidding me? What are you going to do with that toy?" She then dropped the jar containing the pixies in the water, and darted for the stairs.

Missy tied a line to an arrow, dove in the water, and shoved the arrow through one of the air holes in the cover. On shore, Tara and Missy pulled the jar out of the water, then broke the jar. The three Pixies lie on the ground coughing and gasping for air. Missy and Tara assisted the pixies to their feet, gave them dry clothes. Ditsy questioned, "Who was that, human with the loose screws in her head?"

"That is Ralph's girlfriend."

"That witch? You have got to be kidding me?"

Mitty asked, "Who's up for some payback?"

Ralph walked up, took the spider out of the water and asked, "Why is Kathleen's pet spider floating in the pond? You sprites better have a straightforward answer or all of you are in trouble."

Tara explained, "That spider almost eat Ditsy. Then it came after us so we roasted the thing. If that wasn't enough, Kathleen, put Misty, Ditsy, and Mitty in a jar and threatened to drown them if I didn't go with her. When I refused, she dropped the jar in the water and took off. It was only by the grace of God that the pixies in the jar didn't die."

"I am so sorry, I don't know how she keeps getting in the house." Ralph locked his eyes on the pixie security team instructed, "You guys go upstairs and keep an eye out on things. Tara and I are going stay here and put our heads together hopefully we can come up some answers."

Tara sat on Ralph's right shoulder and asked, "Where to from here?"

"I was thinking about going to Kathleen's house and talk to her, maybe we can talk some sense into her."

"How about if the security team threaten to her perfect her butt with a couple dozen arrows if she doesn't stop harnessing us."

"Violence never solved anything Tara, besides Kathleen would have the police after us."

"What is she going to say? Four pixies threatened her? I don't think so."

"Let me make some tea then we will discuss this further."

"Could you make some Cinnamon tea?"

Ten minutes later, Ralph gave Tara a mug of Cinnamon tea. Took a sip of hers, then she handed Ralph a small pair of bathing trunks.

"Ralph glanced at them and inquired, "What is this for?"

Tara smiled at Ralph as he quickly shrunk, she then said, "It's time you and I had some fun. Give me a minute to go in the house, put my bathing suit on, then we'll enjoy ourselves on the water slide."

An hour later, Ralph cuddled up to Tara by the campfire and kissed her on her lips. Tara smiled, and said, "I'm going to go in the house and get dress. Why don't you come in and keep me company?"

The next morning, a depressed Ralph, walked out of the house with Tara's robe on and sat by the water with his head down.

Tara sat next to him in a short, red, and gold kimono, put her hand on his back and asked, "Are you alright, Hon?"

"Leave me alone."

"Are you angry with me because mated last night?"

"No. I am mad at myself for enjoying being in bed with you last night."

"It was my fault too. I shrunk you with the hopes that we could snuggle. But, when things began to happen, I was enjoying it way too much to stop you. Thank you for showing me that you love me."

"We are Christians and should have waited until after we were married to do that."

"Let me put it this way. I wanted it too. But, remember, if we claim that we are without sin, we are fooling ourselves and the truth is not in us. But, when we confess our sins to Christ. He will forgive us our sins."

Ralph stared at Tara smiling sweetly, pushed her on her down and snuggled up to her side and said, "Thank you."

Chapter 10

CONFRONTATION

The next day, Ralph was back to his normal size, put Tara on his right shoulder saying, "I have to get some small clothes so when you shrink me again, I have something to wear."

Upstairs, Missy reported, "All clear, Sir."

"If I gave you an address do you think you and your girls can get there without being seen?"

"Is Alaska known as the land of the midnight sun?"

"Good, now, give me a few minutes and I'll whip us up a hearty breakfast."

A short time later, Ralph served the five Pixies apple pancakes with bits of sausages and tiny mugs of tea. He then stated, "This is the plan. I will call Kathleen and tell her that I need to meet at her place so we can talk. Tara, you will be in Emma's backpack. Missy, you lead your group to the address I give you."

"What if she denies that she was here?" asked Tara.

"I found her earring when you and I were talking. Which will prove that she was here. Plus, not many people around here have a Goliath Spider as a pet."

Ditsy inquired, "Are you going to tell us what you two talked about last night?"

"I just told you the outcome of our conversation."

"Oh. Okay. You spent some personal time with Tara."

"Missy! Give me ten flights around the living room for that remark!"

"But Sir? I was just curious."

"I said do it now! Not next week!"

"Yes, Sir."

An hour later, at Kathleen's log cabin ranch, Ralph whispered, "You okay Tara? Knock twice if you are ready." Ralph glanced at the trees surrounding the place, to make sure Missy and her girls were in position. Kathleen opened the door with a smile on her face, gave Ralph a hug saying, "It is so nice to see you, why don't you come in and I'll put on a pot of coffee."

Ralph stepped inside, slowly scanned the dark blue living room with pictures of bats, spiders, and a pair of Pixie wings mounted over the fireplace. Ralph glared at the wings and complained, "You have got to be kidding? Those Pixie wings look gross hanging up there, and when did you paint your place so dark and gruesome?"

"You don't like the way I redecorated the place? I think my trophy Pixie wings hanging over the fireplace looks great."

"How could you? That's like hanging up someone's arms on your wall."

"Oh, come on. It's not like they are intelligent beings. What do you like in your coffee?"

Kathleen sat on a dark gray couch, served Hazelnut coffee with a platter of pastry to Ralph who sat in a comfortable chair across from her, and stated, "I do not like you coming in my home, and harassing Tara."

"Who said I was there?"

"You want proof?" Ralph went to his car for a package, put it in front of Kathleen and opened it saying, "I found your spider, George dead, in my basement and you dropped your earring when you were trying to kill Tara's security guards."

"I may like the creatures of the night, but I wouldn't kill the pixies who live in your home."

"What is it about Tara that fascinates you so much? Are you jealous over a twelve-inch tall woman? Or is your heart so cold that you don't care who you cause to suffer."

"I told you that sprites are insects, no more, no less. So, all I am going to do is selling an insect to the lab."

"You are so wrong Kathleen!"

An enraged Tara flew out of the backpack, hovered above Ralph's head and screamed, "How dare you call my people insects! If I were a few feet taller I'd beat that living snot out of you, you poor excuse for a human!"

"Big talk coming from an insect."

Tara spotted the wings hanging on the wall, flew up to them and cried, "Why? The Pixie that they belonged to did nothing to hurt you." Tara let go a scream and tried to attack Kathleen.

Ralph held the pixie in his hand and stated, "There is your proof that Tara and her people are sentient beings, they have a spontaneous emotional response to your evil."

Kathleen inquired sweetly, "Ralph Honey, have you sent out the wedding invitations yet?"

"I am calling the wedding off because you love darkness rather than light, and I am taking those pixie wings."

"But Sweetheart, why are you calling off our wedding when we mean so much to each other."

"I'm beginning to see a side of you that I do not want any part of and you are more like a leech than a human being."

"Honey, don't be so quick to act. Maybe we can work things out."

"I don't think you understand what I am saying. So, let me put it this way. If you were that last woman on Earth, I would shoot you."

Kathleen reached under a couch pillow, took hold of a western style six shooter, pointed it at Ralph saying, "Hand over the pixie and I won't shoot you."

Ralph smiled then said, "Drop the gun Kathleen, because right now there are four pixie sharpshooter pointing their crossbows at you."

"All I see is you and that insect you call, Tara."

Missy stood on the fireplace mental, leveled her crossbow at Kathleen and ordered, "Drop the pea shooter or I'll drop you."

"What? You are gonna stick me with that thing you call a crossbow? Not today."

Misty stood on one end of the couch, Ditsy on the other end with Mitty, hovering four feet in front of her. Ralph stated, "What about four little arrows sticking in your miserable hide." Ralph glanced at Tara and said, "Get those wings and we are out of here."

As Tara put her hands on the wings, Kathleen fired a shot that nicked her right shoulder. Suddenly four arrows embedded themselves in Kathleen, she fell to the floor screaming and writhing in pain. Missy hovered just above Kathleen's face and informed, "I forgot to tell you. We dip our arrows in a salt solution. Oh, a bit of warning, you show your ugly face around Ralph's place again. Our next arrows will be dipped in deadly poison."

Tara stood on Kathleen's chest, blew a lilac powder in her face and said, "That is little something to remind you of what will be in store for you if you come around again. Oh, a word of advice, don't move for a good hour. Because when you do, you will get violently nauseous. Later."

Ralph stood over Kathleen and inquired, "One more thing. Where is the pixie called Peppy?"

"Go suck an egg Loser! She then closed her eyes moaning and pleaded, "Ralph, please help me, I am so sick."

He placed a cold wet towel on her forehead and instructed, "Don't move for an hour and you will be alright."

Missy ordered, "Alright girls, we don't leave any evidence behind so remove your arrows from her."

In the car, Tara grumbled, "Way to go Ralph. We were there to send Kathleen a message to back off. But, you had to cave in and put a towel on her forehead."

"A little bit of kindness goes a long way. Remember that."

Ralph parked his car in the parking lot of Specialty Laboratories forty-five minutes later. Looked up at the three-story silver saucer, shaped building resting on four square pillars with an elevator in the center. Ralph put on the knapsack with Tara in it and entered the building and exited the elevator, in a futuristic environment. A young woman approached him and asked, "Can I be of any assistance, Sir?"

"Yes, I would like to speak to the half-wit that runs this place."

A tall man in his fifties with salt and pepper hair clad in a white lab coat walked by. The woman caught his attention and stated, "This gentleman would like to speak to the head half-wit."

The man glared at the woman and said, "That will be all Marla." He looked at Ralph and asked, "Are you here for the free tour?"

"No. I am here to talk some sense into that thick skull of yours."

"You lost me, son. Please elaborate."

Ralph showed him the flyer and asked, "How could you experiment on those poor creatures?"

"There must be some mistake. That's our Logo, but Specially Labs never printed that advertisement. "We deal strictly in agriculture. If there were such things as pixies. This lab would do everything in its power to stop the ones who wanted to hurt them."

Tara shot out of the backpack, sat on Ralph's right shoulder, leaned forward saying, "Words are cheap. How many of my people have you experimented on already?"

The man slowly stretched out his hand saying, "Hi, I'm Stan. And you are ma'am?"

Ralph spoke, "This is Tara, my friend who I am trying to keep out of your lab."

"Let me take you on a tour."

On the first floor, Stan showed Ralph what they were doing to improve livestock feed without using chemicals or growth hormones. Then on the second floor, Stan showed Ralph what the lab was doing to improve a heartier wheat, and corn crops. Then on the third floor, Stan explained that's where everything came together. He then inquired, "Would you mind if I take a closer look at your pixie friend?"

"If it is alright with Tara."

Tara flew off Ralph's shoulder, lit on a stainless-steel table, looked up at Stan with her hands on her posterior and said, "Look away but, keep those probes where I can see them."

"Nice dress. Could you remove it so I can have a look at your wings?"

An embarrass Tara stood motionless in her underwear and stated firmly, "Don't even think of asking me to remove any else."

Stan put Tara under large magnifying glass and muttered, "The way your wings are attached to your back is so fantastic. It's just like the other one, you are a miniature human in every sense of the word."

Tara felt a small metal probe touch high up on her inner thigh, she squealed, spun around and said "Hey that's too close to my you know what! You have seen more of me than I wanted to see, this exam is over."

"Sorry Pixie. I would act the same way if I were in your shoes."

"Come to our place and I can arrange for you to have the same treatment you just gave me."

With Tara dressed, Ralph asked, "What do you mean just like the other one?"

"A slip of the tongue that's all."

Ralph bragged, "You are looking at a Pixie that deals in drugs and knows what spices and herbs to put in what catalyst. She can shrink people, make them grow, cause them to have memory loss, there is an herb that will cause instant paralysis when blown in the face."

Stan thought for a minute then stated, "That could be the reason why someone is after your pixie. Think about it. With the ability to shrink and crawl in a mail slot, disable guards, then return to normal and rob the place blind. Or use that knowledge to change someone's' mind who is in political power." Stan stared at Tara and said, "That little lady has all that power at her fingertips."

"I can do that and a whole lot more." stated Tara, "However as a Pixie Druggist, I am sworn to use my knowledge to help Pixies everywhere."

Ralph stated, "The one who is after Tara has to be a Pixie because only pixies know what Tara is."

Tara stated, "My friend Peppy is still unaccounted for, so, whoever has her is the one after me which maybe Kathleen."

"Kathleen may be a pain in the neck but she is no crook." stated Ralph.

Back in Ralph's car, Tara stood on the dashboard with her hands on her hips and growled, "When are you going to get it through that thick head of yours that Kathleen is out to line her pockets with money any way she can."

"You have her all wrong," stated Ralph, "Because Kathleen is a Christian and would not do something like that."

"Kathleen's walk with Christ is debatable if you ask me."

"You don't know her the way I do."

"Apparently not because we found a pair of Pixie wings pinned to her wall. That says exactly where she stands."

"She could have bought them from a friend."

"Who did Kathleen get them from? Her loser friend Frank? That guy doesn't have the brains to plan an elaborate scheme like this."

"You could be right, he is a few flowers short of a garden."

"A few flowers short? All he has in his garden are weeds."

"Did you have a chance to look around the lab?"

"They are on the up and up. By the way, did you see that metal probe Stan was gonna put up my, oh never mind, you won't understand anyway."

"I am sorry that I suggested the exam. But you didn't have to show him your bare butt."

"Stan was the one who pulled my undies down, not me."

"Sorry I didn't know that."

"Then pay attention the next time a human wants to give me a physical exam. I would have been hurting big time if he stuck that big cold metal thing up my hum."

"Wanna hug?" asked Ralph.

"I think I need one right now."

Ralph folded his arms across his chest, Tara stood on his arms and gave him a long hug saying, "Please don't let anything happen to me."

"What do you say we pay Frank a visit?"

"As soon as I put something in my belly."

Chapter 11

ANOTHER GUEST

Tara stared at Ralph and said, "It's time that I made myself your size again. Find a gas station."

At the gas station, Ralph tossed Tara's clothes in the women's room, she inhaled the black powder, exited the restroom, stretched and said, "Lord, it feels so good to be tall again."

Ralph gave Tara a kiss, then entered the burger joint. A short man by the name of Mack approached him and said, "Ralph, where have you been keeping yourself and who is this lovely lady holding your arm."

"This is Tara Jones."

"If you will excuse me for saying. Kathleen looks like a hideous piece of flesh compared to her. Hey, does she have a sister and you could introduce me to her?"

"Nope, she is an only child."

Tara stared at Mack for ten seconds before saying, "Before you leave here, call a road service to have your right front tire fixed, it's about to blow."

"I just had them put on last week."

"There is a weak spot on the inside wall of the front tire."

Twelve minutes later, Ralph and Tara sat in a booth enjoying their meal. Mack walked up to them and asked, "Tara. how did you know that my tire had a huge bulge in it?"

Ralph stated, "Sir, I want to ask you a few questions."

Mack threw up his hands saying, "Whatever it is I didn't do it."

"Relax, all I want to ask you is. Have you heard of anyone selling authentic fairy wings?"

"That's a strange subject. But, what is stranger is, yes, I have. Your Ex-girlfriend supposed to have bought some from a guy Frank hangs around with. But, for the life of me, I can't think of his name."

Ralph gave Mack ten dollars saying, "Thank you and stay out of trouble for once in your life."

Back in Ralph's car, he stated, "I know we have twenty-four hours before you shrink so what do you want to do?"

"This time, I have forty-eight hours which is the max I can stay this size. Now let's go find that loser, Frank."

Ralph and Tara entered a gin mill called 'The Purple Cat,' sat next to Frank nursing a beer, handed him a picture of himself and said, "Kathleen dropped this in my living room. I thought that you might want to give it back to her."

"You know about Katy and me?"

"It's not a well-kept secret. Oh, by the way, I had my bathrobe fumigated after you wore it."

"If the only thing you came in here is to insult me. Then, leave before you are thrown out."

"Kathleen bought a pair of Pixie Wings. Do you know who she bought them from?"

"Why? You want a pair too?"

"I just want to know where the person is that sold them to her."

Frank put his right hand on Tara's hip saying, "I tell you what. You let me have this lovely lady for an evening and I will tell you where you can find the man that sole Kathleen the Pixie Wings."

"No deal."

"Look around you, then think, what would happen to you if I call for help. Now, do I have a deal or are you going to the hospital."

Tara touched Ralph's right arm saying, "I'll see you outside."

"But Tara, you don't know what he wants from you."

"There is only one way out of this dilemma and that is to give him what he deserves. So, go, I'll meet you in the car in a few minutes."

Ralph leaned against his car, with a landslide of images rushing

73

through his mind of Tara being sexually abused by Frank. However, six minutes later, Tara merrily approached Ralph and said, "Shall we go."

"What happened?"

"Frank decided to take a nap. What, did you think I was going to do? Give in to his lewd desires? No way was I going to do it with that Slime Ball. I'm yours and there is no way you are going to get out of it." Tara paused for a moment, then said, "Wait a minute. It just dawned on me. When Stan had me under his glass, he stated, "It's just like the other ones. My guess is he has Peppy.""

Back at Specially Labs parking lot, Tara placed her hand on Ralph's chest saying, "Wait. Before we go inside. Let's check the flowerbeds to see if Peppy has escaped."

"You take the right side of the parking lot and I'll search on the left side. If Peppy is around here we will find her."

An hour and forty minutes later, Ralph shook his head and said, "I am sorry Tara, I searched everywhere and no Peppy."

"I know she is here. We have to look header this time."

Ralph pointed to the center divider of the parking lot and said, "She could be hiding in the Sweet Williams that are around the trees."

At the third tree from the left, Ralph hollered, "I Found her!"

Tara knelt, gently parted the flowers, and saw a one foot tall, tattered, unconscious pixie lying face down in the dark brown mulch. Tara asked, "Ralph, give me your hanky, then find me two sturdy branches just over a foot long. Tara fashioned a makeshift stretcher, put Peppy on it, then brought her to the car.

"What do you have there!" hollered the security guards. Tara gave the stretcher to Ralph, reached in her purse as the guard approached and stated, "That pixie escaped from Specially Labs several days ago. So, hand her over."

Tara stated, "I don't think so. What are you gonna do? Tell the police that we stole a sprite? They'd laugh I your face."

The guard pointed his gun at them saying, "Give me the pixie and I won't shoot."

Tara blew a small amount of brown powder in the guard's face then stated, "Put your gun away and return to your post. Because all you found is a pixie doll that a little girl lost." Tara glanced at Ralph saying,

"Give me Peppy and let's get out of here before that suggestive powder wears off."

In Ralph's home, the security pixie gathered around as Tara paced Peppy on a folded hand towel in the kitchen. Then told Ralph, "Get me that thing that you put on someone's forehead to tell their temperature."

Tara stared at the pixie's temperature reading in unbelief, and said, "Ralph you get her clothes off, while I fill the sink with cold water. We have to get her temperature down."

Once Peppy's fever was down, Tara gave her White Willow for the fever, and Turmeric mixed with Black Pepper to fight inflammation. Tara then gently rolled Peppy on her stomach, prepared her wing stubs, then asked, "Ditsy, did you soak the wings in the solution the way I told you?"

"Yes."

"Good. Get them. Then scrub up because you are going to play doctor and perform a win graft."

Ditsy put her hands out in front of her saying, "No, no, no, no, no, no, no, no. I'm all thumbs and I'll botch it up."

"I know you can do it now go downstairs and put five scoops of Scarlet Infusion into a clean glass container, then put a small crystal in a mortar then use the pestle to grind it to powder. Add that to the Scarlet with three drops of the thick, dark brown Oak Tree Sap. If you mixed everything right, the solution should turn clear."

Ditsy returned ten minutes later with the clear liquid. Tara then instructed Ditsy to apply the clear liquid to each wing stub, and suture the wing to each the stub."

With Peppy bandaged and in Tara's bed resting comfortable, Tara patted Ditsy's back saying, "Congratulations. You just performed your first wing graft. Now, the rest is in the Lord's hands."

"Will Peppy have the use of her wings again?"

"Time will tell. But I am sure when Peppy wakes she will be flying again in no time." Tara looked at Missy and said, "I want you to set up a 24-hour watch on Peppy. Misty, Ditsy, and Mitty each take an eight-hour shift. Talk to you later."

Tara met Ralph on the back deck, sat in a recliner next to him and asked, "Do you want to go back to the lab and tell Stan that we found a seriously injured pixie on this property?"

"Sort of rubbing it in his face? Sure, why not. But I want to wait until Peppy is better."

Kathleen walked in the backyard with a chocolate cake, waved with a bright smile saying, "Hi guys!"

Tara whispered, "That woman doesn't give up does she."

"Be nice."

"How do you be pleasant to someone that's kin to a Piranha? The last time we met she tried to kill Misty, Ditsy, Missy, and Mitty. What do you say I shrink her, put her in a bottle and drop her in the water?"

"Tara!" growled Ralph.   Kathleen walked on the back deck, handed Ralph the cake saying, "I was a little out of line earlier, will you forgive me?" She stared at Tara for several seconds before saying, "I never knew pixies could change sizes the way you do."

"Only those who understand pharmaceutics can."

Kathleen pulled up a chair, sat next to Tara and inquired, "Is what you do sorcery?"

"Far from it. There are herbs and spices that need a catalyst to trigger right response and you humans don't know anything about them."

"Fascinating. Could you tell me more about your profession as a Pixie Druggist? Like how do you make yourself big and how long does it last?"

"Black powder makes me big, and is a combination of a ton of ingredient that is aged in a cave for three years before it can be used. The length of time depends on how much is used. Being a Pharmacy Pixie is very tricky, I could mix crimson spice with the fire mushroom and indigo, put that in the catalyst like coffee, the person intelligence would increase a hundred-fold. But, if I put that same stuff in Earl Grey tea, the person would be dumb as a stump. You know that lilac powder that I blew in your face that made you sick." If I put that spice in tea, you'd hook up with the first man you saw and jump his bones all night."

"Could you show me where you keep your herbs?"

"No. That's a trade secret." Tara then asked, "Ralph, Sweet, could you and Kathleen make a pot of coffee so we can have it without cake?"

As soon as Kathleen was in the house, Tara opened Kathleen's pocketbook, took the tape out of her mini tape recorder, and hid it."

Ten minutes later, Kathleen served cake and coffee then inquired, "Would it be possible if you could give me back the pixie wings that I paid a bundle for?"

Tara smiled and said, "Sorry no can do. They are on a pixie."

Kathleen almost dropped her mug of coffee, then asked, "How is that possible?"

"A simple wing graft, any Pixie Druggist can do that."

"How do you know those wigs belong to Peppy"

"I don't. Every wing pattern is different. Just like your fingerprints are different."

"Then you owe me fifty thousand dollars. Because that is how much I am out."

"It's not my fault that you bought stolen property you dumb idiot."

"Pixie wings, dragonfly wings, what's the difference? They are both unintelligent arthropods."

Tara took a swallow of her coffee, stood to her feet, and said, "Dragonfly wings will not work on a sprite, and I am not a stupid insect!"

"No." replied Kathleen sheepishly.

Tara unzipped the back of her dress, allowing her wings to show. Then asked, "What about now?"

Kathleen stared at Tara's wings sticking above her head and remained silent.

Tara grabbed Kathleen by her waist and was about to take off with her when Ralph hollered, "Ladies, back off, before someone gets hurt. Tara, I'd tuck your wings in before someone sees you." Ralph turned to Kathleen and asked, "Who sold you those pixie wings?"

"I can't divulge that information."

Can you show me this so called Peppy?"

"Under one condition, Peppy stays where she is."

Downstairs, in front of Tara's home, she warned, "Look in the window on the right. But just remember, my security team has three poised arrows pointed at your head."

Kathleen knelt, and looked in the window at Peppy lying in a dou' bed, and said, "She doesn't look life like."

When Peppy heard Kathleen's voice, she began to scream and thrash around her bed. Missy ordered, "Mitty, Misty help. She then ordered, "You, human, it is time for you to leave."

Kathleen rose to her feet, looked Tara in her eyes saying, "You accuse me of having stolen property when you are guilty of the very thing."

"I've never stolen anything in my whole life."

"You are a thief and a liar! You stole Ralph from me, you little Hussy."

"If you don't know how to keep a man that's not my problem. Now, go back upstairs like you were told."

Kathleen handed Ralph two hundred dollars saying, "I am renting the bedroom on the first floor. Now, there is no way you can legally throw me out."

"You just can't move in when we are not married."

"Excuse me? You have six pixies living with you and one of them is six feet tall. One more female will not make a difference."

"Okay but the basement is off limits to you. So, upstairs or Tara's guards will use you for target practice."

Chapter 12

TARA GETS EVEN

Kathleen brought her stuff in from the car and quickly unpacked. Then called someone on her cell phone saying, "I'm in and I have good news. Not only does he have six pixies living in his basement, he has the one that knows all about the herbs and spices they use."

"You're in there to do what you are told to do, which means no fooling around with Ralph is that clear."

"The thought never entered my mind. Love you."

With Ralph in the basement, Kathleen sat at the dining room table drinking a mug of coffee. Tara sat across from her with a cup of tea and commented, "My, that's a pretty low-cut blouse you have on." glancing up at Ditsy sitting on the chandelier.

"All's fair in love and war and I plan to use what I have to win Ralph back, so, a word to the wise, start packing Pixie."

Tara smiled politely then nodded. Ditsy dropped a black fuzzy object down the front of Kathleen's blouse then took off. Tara jumped to her feet shouting, "Ohmigosh! Was that a big spider that just dropped between your boobies!" Kathleen then screamed, tore off her top, danced around screaming, "Get off me, get it off me!"

Tara picked up the ball of black fuzz saying, "Gotcha. It is amazing how easy it is to fool you, humans. See ya. I'm gonna check on my Honey downstairs."

As soon as the basement door was closed, Kathleen went in the den to search for the penny and Tara's hidden herbs but came up short.

Later, Ralph approached Kathleen and stated, "Tara and I are going for a walk be back in twenty minutes. Kathleen took a bobby pin, went to the basement door, and tried to pick the lock. But as soon as she touched the doorknob, she let go a scream as flew back against the wall. Because Misty and Mitty who were on the other side of the door sent a powerful charge of electricity through the doorknob.

Kathleen shook her head, and staggered to her feet as Ralph and Tara entered the house. Ralph stared at Kathleen's hair standing on end, snickered, and said, "The frizzed outlook went out of style years ago."

Kathleen reached up and felt her hair that was standing up, then stated, "Oh shut up." and stormed off to her room.

Ralph glanced at Tara and inquired, "Is there something going on that you are not telling me?"

"I'm acting like a normal pixie and giving Kathleen every opportunity to make a fool of herself that's all."

"Tara, what does that mean?"

Tara smiled devilishly and said, "Ohhh, not much."

Later, Kathleen walked up to Ralph, clad in a thin slinky burgundy dress, made a cup of tea for Tara then put some sedative in it, and served it to her with some pastry. After a few sips, Tara quickly retired to the basement for the evening. Kathleen put on some soft Chopin, turned the lights down low, then invited Ralph to join her on the couch.

As soon as Kathleen put her arms around Ralph to kiss him. She let go a bloodcurdling scream then fell on the floor in pain, because a large staple was shot in her left butt cheek.

Ralph knelt saying, "It's a big staple. Hold still so I can pull them out."

"So, help me I'm gonna kill those Pixies."

With the staples out, Ralph assisted Kathleen on her feet and said, "You get yourself ready, while I get the hydrogen peroxide and the bandages."

"Don't bother," grumbled Kathleen, "I'll do it myself." went in her room and slammed the door.

Ralph looked at the couch and saw his staple gun wedged between the back of the sofa and pillow. Wondered, *"What in the world is that doing there."* When he pulled it out, Ditsy was holding unto the trier.

She smiled sheepishly saying, "I found this and didn't know where to put it. I heard Kathleen holler. Is she hurt?"

"You stapled her left butt check."

Ditsy snickered, "I bet that hurt."

"Go see what you can do to help Kathleen Ditsy."

Ditsy pounded on Kathleen's bedroom door saying, "I'm sorry I hurt your butt. Can I help make it better?"

"Go away you little Imp! I don't need your kind of help!"

"I have something that will take away the pain."

"Alright come in."

"Are you gonna put me in a bottle like last time?"

"No."

Ditsy flew to the dresser, and said, "Remove your dress, expose your fanny, then lay on the bed."

Ditsy flew to the bed, patter Kathleen's tush saying, "Those staple marks look nasty." then she put some green pain revealing ointment on it and bandaged it.

Kathleen quickly rolled over, grabbed Ditsy saying, "Now I have got you." then stood up.

Ditsy smiled and said, "Not today human." pulled a stickpin from the back of her shirt, rammed it in Kathleen's finger. She screened as she let go of the pixie.

Ditsy flew just outside the bedroom door, stopped, wiggled her butt saying, "Come and get me if you can. Uh oh." she then swiftly dropped down as a big dictionary hit the wall in the hall. Ditsy then stuck her tongue out and said, "You missed me." then flew away.

Ralph walked down the hall, locked his gaze on Kathleen and inquired, "What's going on here?"

"Oh, shut up." grumbled Kathleen as she slammed the door.

Ralph opened the door and stated, "If you are going to be staying here. You have to act civil or I will toss you out on your pretty little butt."

"Tell that to those imps you call friends."

"Throwing books at them after they helped you isn't the right way to make friends. But I'll talk to Tara to tell her guards to draw back."

Ralph sat next to Tara sleeping on the grass, tapped her shoulder.

She quickly sat up, and said, "Ralph help me. I can hear you but my eyes are still in my dream."

When Tara's head cleared she held Ralph stating, "I just had the dream where I was being held by a bunch of men in a dark room who were deciding kill me. I flew through a window, then ran into a barn close by. Inside, I climbed the wall on my right to a shelf where I lay flat on my back but they found me. Fearing for my life, I crawled on my hands and knees along the shelf into another room, and suddenly woke from my sleep. I heard you and felt your hand touching me, but my eyes were still locked in the dream and I could not see you." A frightened Tara held Ralph with tears in her eyes saying, "I was scared that I was going blind."

"You're stressed out from trying to keep Kathleen from capturing you. But, you're gonna have to back off on Kathleen."

"She told me that she was going to use her female charm to win you back and if that happened, Only His Divine Intervention will stop me from seeking my revenge."

"You do not want to go down that path because it will only lead to your destruction." warned Ralph. He then answered his cellphone saying, "It's your dime. Oh, hi Kathleen. What do you want?"

"My left leg is bothering me. Can you come upstairs and help me?"

Ralph looked at Tara and said, "Gotta go. Kathleen needs me."

Upstairs, Ralph approached Kathleen in her bedroom dressed in a dark blue bath towel. She smiled sweetly and said, "Could you be a dear and help walk me to the shower? My left thigh hurts really bad."

In the bathroom, Kathleen was ready to remove her towel to entice Ralph in the shower with her. When she saw Tara standing in the open bathroom door with a small crossbow pointing at her head. She glanced at Ralph and said, "Thank you, I ah, can take it from here." and stepped into the shower, closed the door then got rid of the towel.

Tara met Ralph in the hall and had a hot mug of coffee and pastry she then escorted him to the dining room table and inquired, "How is Kathleen doing?"

Suddenly nightmarish screams followed by someone pounding on a wall caught Ralph's attention. Tara touched his hand saying, "I'll go see what's wrong." Tara entered the bathroom and asked, "Are you alright in there?"

"The water is stuck on ice cold and the shower door is jammed. Can you get Ralph before I freeze to death?"

"He is busy right now. Can I help?"

"Go down stairs and turn off the stupid water you Halfwit!"

"Say please."

"So, help me when I get out of this shower I am going to flatten you! Now, turn off the water!" screamed Kathleen.

Tara tossed Kathleen her towel saying, "Hold this up between you and the water."

Ten minutes later, a shivering Kathleen walked out of the shower, wrapped a dry towel around her, glanced at Ralph who just entered and stated, "You spineless coward. You let that Imp turn the hot water off on me, then you do nothing about it. Well I am going to put a stop to it right now." Kathleen went to deck Tara, she caught her fist in her right hand, twisted it, then cold-cocked her.

Ralph helped Tara lay Kathleen on her bed, Tara then instructed, "It's lady's only from here."

With Ralph gone, Tara slapped Kathleen across the face, until she opened her eyes, glared down at Kathleen said, "You can stay in my home under one condition. You keep your hands off my mate, Ralph."

"This place belongs to the man I am going to marry and no Imp is going to stand in my way!" screamed Kathleen in defiance.

"The pixie's law states, what belongs to the Pixie's mate is hers also." Tara got in Kathleen's face saying, "If you wake up one morning on the front lawn naked, you'll know I mean business. So, stay away from my mate!"

"What do you mean, your mate?" screamed Kathleen.

"We mated in my bed a few days ago. Now, he is mine and I will fight to the death to keep him. Oh, the next time you try kissing Ralph I'll use the nail gun instead." Tara turned to leave, Kathleen picked up a heavy object to hit her on the back of the head. Tara's eyes turned red as she let go a shriek, picked Kathleen by her shoulders, and slammed her against the wall ready to put an end to her.

Ralph charged in the room and hollered, "Don't do it Tara!"

"She wants to take you away from me and I am going to put a stop to all this right now."

"Tara, listen to me, no one is going to turn my heart away from you. So, please put Kathleen down."

Tara let Kathleen fall to the floor, turned, and walked out of the room. Ralph picked up the bath towel, handed it Kathleen, turned around saying, "Please cover yourself."

"Now, what's this I hear about you and that insect having sex?" inquired Kathleen.

"Before I answer your question, I found Frank's undershorts in my bed which tells me what Tara said about you and him doing it, is true. So, put your clothes on."

Kathleen put her arms around Ralph and said, "What do you say we make that imp jealous."

Ralph pushed her away saying "Get a life will ya. We're Christians, or have you forgotten that." he then walked out of the room.

Ralph found Tara sitting on the back deck with her head down. He sat next to her and asked, "Are you going to be alright?"

"I am so sorry, don't know why I acted like that."

"You wanna tell me how the hot water was turned off during Kathleen's shower?"

"You know how us pixies are. We like playing around and things got out of hand."

"You wanna hold back on the teasing, someone may get hurt."

Tara snickered, "You should have told me before I set that blue powder trap in her closet."

"You didn't, please tell me you didn't"

"I would but that would be a lie."

Kathleen stormed on the back deck in her underpants, covered in blue powder and said, "When are you going to put a leash in that pet of yours? Now I have to take another shower provided there is hot water."

Tara warned, "Don't use water, that will only cause the powder to stain your skin blue. You should use talcum-powder to remove it."

Five minutes later, a nude Kathleen stormed on the back deck all blue and screamed, "Very funny, very funny. You knew that I wouldn't listen to you. so, you told me the truth. Now, how do I get this stuff off me?"

Tara snickered, "You look just like one of the Na`vi people on Pandora."

"Can the cryptic remarks and tell me how I get this stuff off me."

"Cooking oil will remove it. But, it has to be headed to your body temperature first. Do you want me to help you?"

"All I want is for you to stay away from me!" screamed Kathleen.

Just then, the pastor walked on the back deck saw Kathleen and said, "Miss Summers, you ought to be ashamed of yourself walking around in public like that."

After Kathleen made a quick exit, Ralph explained, "She is having one of those days where everything is going wrong."

"Including painting herself blue, then run around bare-naked?"

"Kathleen stumbled into an open bag of blue dye and she was so upset that she forgot about putting some clothes on when she came out here to ask Tara's advice. Hey, can I get you a cup of coffee?"

"I came here to tell you that Kathleen Summers still plans to go through with the wedding."

"I don't know how we are going to get married without a marriage license."

"But Miss Summers showed me the marriage license right after I met you and Tara."

"It's probably forged."

"You two are going to have to get together on your wedding plans." The pastor glanced at Tara, then said, "I'll leave a date open, two weeks from today. Please let me know one way or the other. See you Sunday morning in church."

Chapter 13

KATHLEEN'S REVENGE

Missy flew up to Ralph all excited and said, "You have got to come downstairs to see this."

In the basement, Ralph walked up behind Peppy clad in a yellow short set, dangling her legs in the water, and he said, "Aren't you the picture of health?"

Peppy squealed, "A human!" fell in the water then tried to swim away. Ralph Picked her up, and said, "Settle down, I'm not going to hurt you. Oh, I'm Ralph and you're in my basement."

Peppy continued to scream, "Please don't hurt me I can't take any more of your testings."

Ralph sat on the grass, held Peppy close to his chest, and began to sing a lullaby. In no time, the terrified pixie was fast asleep. Ralph gently put the sleeping Sprite on the grass, called Tara's security guards and stated, "If Kathleen comes down here, you know she is up to no good so shoot to kill. Tara and I are going to the Specialty Labs to talk to Stan." Ralph woke Peppy and inquired, "Would you like come with me and Tara to Specialty Labs? I want to find the person that hurt you and make him pay, I promise no one will harm you."

Peppy nodded yes, stepped on Ralph's hand then walked up his arm to sit on his shoulder.

Upstairs, Peppy took one look at Tara and exclaimed, "Whoa aren't we the big one! Let's go kick someone's butt." Ralph put Peppy in the special knapsack and headed for the car.

In the lab, Ralph and Tara approached Stan, shook his hand saying, "I believed you when you told me that you didn't experiment on pixies and you had no idea where Peppy was."

Tara put a nervous Peppy on Stan's desk, and Ralph stated, "Look what Tara and I found in Specialty Lab's parking lot, beaten with her wings cut off. Care to explain?"

"You say that you found her on this property, but how do I know you are telling me the truth."

"You can check with the guard on duty that day, and if you examine Peppy's wings you will see that they were reattached."

Stan looked at the pixie and said, "Take off your top so I can get a better look at your wings."

"In your dreams Creep, you get no free peeks from this pixie." Peppy turned around saying, "If you weren't so caught up on kinky stuff you would have noticed that I am wearing a tank top."

Stan took a magnifying glass examined Peppy's wings and said, "This doesn't prove that she was held here against her will. Oh, a nice wing graft, but will they work."

Peppy hunched over, gritted her teeth, and slowly flapped her wings. She stared Stan in his eyes and asked, "You have any more negative statements so I can call you a liar, a cheat, and a deceiver? If you want I can describe the basement lab to you in every detail."

"That's where you are wrong. There is no basement lab here." "Yeah, there is."

"Look, I don't have time to stand here and argue with an insect. Get out of my lab before I have you thrown out."

Peppy picked up a fountain pen and was about to throw it at Stan like a spear, Tara grabbed her and put her in the knapsack, Peppy poked her head out, glared at Stan and stated, "My people are not insects. We have two legs like humans, ergo, we must me miniature humans."

"Get out of my lab!"

In Ralph's car, Peppy climbed out of the backpack, opened her hand, and said, "This is a button from my blouse."

"Where did you get that?"

"On Stan's desk."

Ralph stopped his car in a park, sat on a bench under a huge shade tree with Tara and Peppy. He sat the pixie on his shoulder saying, "Don't judge all humans by Stan or the one who abused you."

"It is difficult to let go of all the horror they put me through the past weeks."

"How did they catch you?"

"I was lying on a huge sunflower in my blouse and shorts trying to get a tan when the lights went out. I opened my eyes sometime later in a wire cage. I screamed and hollered for what seemed like an hour. When somebody with long straight black hair in their late thirties opened my cage, took me out and strapped me face down on a small table. I asked what are you going to do with me? That's when I felt a sharp pain in the upper part of my back and I screamed, "No, please don't cut my wings off! Please don't! I then blacked out from the excruciating pain. I woke back in my cage with a bandage around my chest and I felt for my wings and was horrified to discover that they weren't there. I curled up in the corner of the cage and cried for the longest time wondering what was going to become of me. When a young lady with short, blond hair, gave me a few pieces of rags so I could fashion some kind of a garment." Peppy smiled as she stated, "The lady that came to my cage every evening was my one ray of hope. The fruit treats that she gave me tasted a whole lot better than that kitty kibble they forced to eat.

I lost track of the number of times a probe was shoved up my butt, and needles shoved in my arms, legs, and stomach. I remember one evening I was huddled in the corner of my cage crying when the same lady came by. She opened my cage and held me. The next day they did a series of tests on me that left me bruised and sore from my head to my toes. As they were putting me back in my cage, I overheard the two men discussing how they were going to dissect me the next day. I was horrified and realized that I was going to die. However, that evening the kind lady came by and talked to me but this time she did something different, she opened my cage door and left. Weak from the lack of proper food and sleep, I summoned all my strength, climbed down the rope she left me and I made my way across the floor. But, I was unable to reach the elevator button so I rigged a grappling hook and climbed up the air vent and made my way to the surface. Too weak to make it across the parking lot, I fell asleep in the flower bed halfway and that's where you found me."

Peppy repeatedly tapped Ralph's neck saying, "That lady who just sat on the rock over there. She is the kind woman that helped me. Quick, quick let's go see her."

Ralph, put Peppy in the knapsack and approached the woman and inquired, "Do you work in the basement of Specialty Labs?"

"Why yes, I do. Not very many people know about that. Are you one of the lab techs?"

Ralph asked, "Tara could you get Peppy for me. I heard that you were kind to one of their captives they were experimenting on."

"I'm not allowed to talk about what they do down there."

"But I will," stated Peppy standing on Tara's shoulder.

"You made it out, good for you!" Oh, I'm Tisha, Tisha Gibson and I work in housekeeping at the underground lab. I have read about pixies all my life but never knew they existed until I saw Peppy caged up like an animal so I had to do something. I waited until the time was right and helped her to escape."

Tara put Peppy in Tisha's hand and said, "My assistant did the wing graft. What do you think?"

"Looking good. How many pixies are there around here?"

"More than you know." Tara turned around, knelt down then unzipped the back of her dress so her wings would show."

Tisha gasped and inquired, "Oh, my. But how did you get so big?"

"I'm a Pixie Druggist."

"That's all you have to tell me. Because that says it all."

"How many of my people have been mutilated by those monsters in the lab?"

"I'm not sure, but, I do know that they are looking for a particular pixie which I think is you, Tara."

Ralph glanced up at the sky and said, "By the look of those clouds, we are gonna have a gully washer in a few minutes. Here is my address and phone number, come on over anytime for coffee and whatever."

No sooner than the words were out of Ralph's mouth when it started to rain. He got the umbrella from the trunk and helped Tara and Peppy in the car. On their way to the car, the sky opened and dropped a deluge of rain and Ralph could hardly see of the road through the rain. So, he pulled to the side of the road until it eased up enough to see to drive. When the rain let up a little, Ralph drove home, helped Tara and Peppy out of the car opened the umbrella and headed for the house. But it started pouring hard again. The wind destroyed the umbrella and they had to make a dash for the house with only one thought on their minds and that was to get into the house where it was dry. Finally inside, soaked to the skin Kathleen nudged Tara aside and toweled down Ralph, trying to take his attention away from the Pixie. Peppy climbed out of the knapsack, stood on Ralph's right shoulder, and shouted, "It's you!"

Kathleen snapped Peppy with the towel knocking her off Ralph's shoulder. Peppy screamed in pain as she tried to use her wings to fly but fell to the floor out cold. Tara rushed to pick up Peppy but as she bent over, Kathleen shoved her so that she fell on top of the Pixie.

Ralph pointed to the front door hollering, "That was uncalled for! Now get out of my house this minute, before I have you thrown out."

"Remember, all I have to do is file a lawsuit and have you thrown out. Or, I call the police and tell them that you have drugs on the premises and when they find your pixies you will have some explaining to do. All you have to do is give me Tara and tell me where she keeps her drugs. Then I'll be out of your hair for good."

"Go suck an egg. I will never give you Tara or any of the pixies."

"What will the pastor say when I tell him that you are living with six women."

"Good point. But are you ready to explain to the Pastor how you weaseled your way into my home? Now, if you look around you, you will see four pixies with their crossbows pointed at you. So, go to your room and stay there until it is time to eat."

"I won't have you arrested if you give me the pixie Tara and her drugs."

"There is a moral law which you are guilty of breaking."

Kathleen screamed as she grabbed her left shoulder then pulled out the small arrow. Her eyes rolled back in her head and collapsed on the living room rug.

Misty landed on Kathleen's back and said, "Sorry, sir, I had to do it. That woman was grating on my nerves."

"Is she dead?"

"No, just asleep."

Ralph turned to Tara and asked, "Is Peppy, alright?"

"Yes. I'll have my guards take Peppy downstairs while I drag Miss Mouthy to her room."

"And no tricks. Now, if you will excuse me I am gonna sit in the recliner and rest."

Tara smiled and stated in mock innocence, "Who me, pull a prank on Kathleen? Never."

In Kathleen's room, Tara got her ready for bed, pulled the covers up. Ditsy crawled out of the AC duct, with Tara's median pouch, and inquired, "What do you want me to do now?"

"Put some red liquid on the end of a straight pin, then make two pricks close together like a spider bite on her arm. The red liquid will leave a mark and cause it to itch. Good. Now give me a needle with the white liquid in it."

Tara took the tiny needle and injected a drug into Kathleen's left shoulder, and explained, "When she wakes up, her left arm will be useless for a day. We will tell her that she has been bitten by a rare dreaded scarlet spider. Then have Missy draw up a nasty looking spider."

Ditsy chuckled and asked, "Why are we doing this to her?"

"One, we have to drive her out of this house, I can't find out why Kathleen wants me and my drugs with her here."

"Money, fame and power are the three desires most humans go after."

"You got that right. But who is behind all this? Now I must tend to my honey. Ralph." Tara walked out in the living room and could not wake him. She then felt a sharp pain to the back of her head then passed out. Coming to sometime later lying in Kathleen's bed in her underwear and heard her saying, "Frank I don't know what is wrong with my arm, but, I need you to tie up that troublesome pixie Tara and keep her out of the way. Then we will round up all the pixies and put them in boxes, and package Tara's drugs for shipping."

"But how are we going to get downstairs to capture them? It's locked"

"Break down the door if we have to."

A short time later, Frank entered the bedroom clad in Ralph's robe, stood by the chest of drawers to disrobe with one thought on his mind.

A groggy Tara sprang out of the bed, grabbed Frank saying, "The only way you can have me is in your dreams." and slammed his head against the dresser knocking him out. She then put him in the bed, gagged him with Kathleen's dirty sock and tied him with Kathleen's pantyhose.

Unable to find her dress in the bedroom, Tara crept out in the hall when Kathleen grabbed her by her wings and pulled saying, "Do as I say or experience pain like you never felt before."

"I will not give you the secret to my drugs." Tara then screamed as Kathleen pushed Tara against the wall with her body, drove a pin her sensitive wing muscle hollering, "Tell me what I want to know!"

"I've taken an oath to give my life to keep the secret of the Pixie's drugs. So, go ahead and kill me." Tara smiled, saying, "The birth mark on Frank's Coccyx is very interesting."

Kathleen spun the pixie around and inquired, "What do you mean by that?"

"Why don't you ask him." stated Tara with a smirk on her face.

"You are lying through your teeth!" hollered Kathleen, then landed a right cross to Tara's face that dazed her for only a moment. Kathleen the hauled Tara to the basement door, kicked it open then threw Tara down the stairs."

Chapter 14

KARMA

Once Kathleen was in the basement, she put on a gas mask then sprayed the Pixy guards with a fine mist that caused them to drop to the ground out cold. With Tara and the pixies out of the way, Kathleen hollered, "Frank, get your lazy butt down here and help me find those drugs!"

When Frank didn't respond, Kathleen stormed upstairs in search of him and found him in her room tied up. She groaned, "I give you a simple task like tying someone up and they knocked out? You are pathetic, when you can't even do that right."

"It's not my fault Tara came up behind me and knocked me out."

"You mean to tell me you can't overpower a frail woman like Tara? When I untie you, get dressed, then come downstairs and help me to locate those drugs." Kathleen then left the room.

Frank dressed, want to the kitchen for a bite to eat before going into the basement. Peppy hollered from the counter, "Hey you, Bug Nuggets, over here!" she then blew hand full of black pepper in his face, then jabbed him with an arrow she found. When Frank stumbled backward, Peppy moved the garbage can in his way so he fell over it and struck his head knocking himself out.

With Peppy's wings working, she rushed to Ralph to see if she could wake him, but couldn't because of the sedative Kathleen put on the towel to dry him off.

In the basement, Peppy freed her friends, one by one and hid them in the bushes. She picked up a crossbow, flew to the roof of Tara's house

93

and shouted at Kathleen, "Hey, Bug Nuggets! You lose something?" then let an arrow fly that struck Kathleen in her left shoulder. Kathleen tried to spray Peppy with the sedative mist, but the Pixie flew to the ceiling and hovered, as Kathleen continued trying to spray the elusive Peppy. She let another arrow fly that struck Kathleen's thigh. When she bent down to remove it. Peppy made a beeline for her gas mask, ripped it off. Kathleen was quickly overcome by the gas and collapsed on the grass out cold.

Groggy from the sleeping gas, Peppy did a nosedive in the pond, then crawled on the mountain and passed out.

Sometime later, Peppy opened her eyes on the grass with Ditsy slapping her face, saying, "Come on girl wake up."

A dazed Peppy stared at an unconscious Kathleen and asked, "Hey I did it! How are the others?"

"Guarding the perimeter. I need you to help me to tie up Kathleen."

"I have a better idea, make some Cinnamon Tea then put in some green herb and white powder in her hot drink."

Ten minutes later, Ditsy and Peppy forced a stunned Kathleen to drink the tea, which shrank her in seconds. Missy found an old hamster cage in the pile of junk, put some wood chips in it tossed Kathleen in it and locked it.

Ditsy approached Tara lying motionless by the bushes, took her pulse saying she is alive but I don't know why she is not responding."

Ralph knelt next to Ditsy, covered Tara with a blanket, saying, "Let me try some smelling salts."

One whiff, Tara coughed, opened her eyes and asked, "Will someone please pull that needle out of my wing muscle. Lord does that hurt."

Ralph glanced around and inquired, "Where is Kathleen? I don't see her anywhere?"

Ditsy showed Ralph the cage with a tiny nude Kathleen in it. He picked it up and stated, "My, my I do say that you have lost a little weight."

Kathleen screamed, "Can the cute remarks and get me some clothes!"

"Do you know you have a cute little tush."

"Will you shut up and get me out of here!"

Ralph took Kathleen out of her cage, dropped her in a bottle, put some holes in the top then tied it to a string saying, "What goes around comes around. Tell me who you and Frank are working for or you go for a swim."

"You can't do that to me! That's murder!"

"All I have to do is feed you to the cat and no more body, now tell me who you are working for and why do you want Tara and her drugs?"

"I have no idea what you are talking about."

Ralph lowered the bottle in the water and watched it float, then questioned, "Why do you want Tara's drugs?"

"I told you that I don't know what you are talking about."

Ralph submerged the bottle until it was one-third full of water, lifted it out and said, "Tell me what I want to know."

Kathleen nervously studied the water level in the jar and stated, "I work alone. Now, let me out of here."

Ralph pushed the bottle under until the water filled the jar up to Kathleen's head. He put the bottle on the grass and said, "You have one more chance to tell me the truth then you sleep in the deep. Or, in your case, you get flushed."

Kathleen stared at Ralph with a forlorn look in her eyes and said, "Please don't do this to me. I love you."

Ralph knocked the bottle in the water and watched Kathleen frantically pound on the bottle as it sunk to the bottom of the pond. Fifteen seconds later he reached in the water, took the bottle out, opened it, and dumped the water and Kathleen on the grass. She coughed for a bit, then looked up at Ralph and stated, "You were going to let me drown weren't you." Kathleen crawled up on Ralph's lap, pulled out his shirt to dry herself, then snuggled in his lap. Ralph picked her up by the back of her neck, held her under the water for ten seconds, then asked, "Your soft soap will not work this time. Who do you work for? Is it Specialty labs?"

"I can't tell you."

Ralph held Kathleen under the water for a little longer, before he let her up. But this time Peppy hung her head and said, "I wasn't going to say anything because I wanted to see her die for what she did to me. Kathleen didn't buy my wings from someone. She was the one who cut them off and she was in the lab every time they experimented on me." Peppy's eyes blazed with anger as she slowly walked up to Kathleen with a knife hidden in her hand. Just as Peppy was going to stab Kathleen, Tara picked up Peppy saying, "Pixie's don't kill someone, no matter how evil they are."

"Sorry, When I saw Kathleen I had flashbacks of all the times she tormented me."

"She's lying!" Screamed Kathleen. "I never worked for Specialty labs in my life."

Ralph called Tisha Gibson and asked, "Hey kiddo. How's things? Peppy and Tara wants to see you again. Do you think you can come over?"

"I'll be there in a jiffy."

"The door is unlocked, so come on in we are in the basement."

Ten minutes later Tisha Gibson walked up to Ralph and exclaimed, "You did all this for them! This is fantastic! Hey, who's the Pixie in the cage?" When Tisha drew closer to the cage, she was shocked to see who it was. Kathleen waved her arms trying to tell Tisha not to say that she knew her. But Tisha stated, "Everyone at the Specialty Labs are wondering where you are."

Ralph asked. "Does Kathleen work at the Labs?"

"Oh yeah, Kathleen has been working there ever since you two bought the house, but she goes by the name of Cathy."

Kathleen hollered, "You big mouth! When I get back to the lab I will have them fire your hide!"

Tisha inquired, "Ralph. How did Cathy get so small?"

Ditsy stated, "I gave her hot Cinnamon Tea, then mixed the green herb and white crystal powder. And there she is."

Tara's eyes opened wide as she inquired, "Ditsy, tell me you didn't use the crystal powder with the yellow specs in it."

"Ahhh, Yeah I think I did. Why?"

"The white crystal powder with the yellow specs might make it permanent. Which means Miss Kathleen Summers is now and always will be a twelve-inch tall pixie without wings."

Kathleen screamed, "Nooooo! I won't accept it I just won't! You're lying! Please tell me that you are lying!"

Tara held the cage up to her face so she could look Kathleen's eyes and said, "When it comes to my drugs, I am always dead serious. You Miss Summers will have to live the rest of your life one foot tall."

Ralph asked, "What are we going to do with her?"

Peppy suggested, "Why don't we donate her to the lab. I am sure they will take good care of her."

"No, you can't do that to me," screamed Kathleen, "I'll, I'll do anything you say just don't send me to the lab."

Ralph saw the terrified look on Kathleen's face and asked, "What are you afraid of?"

"Any pixie that goes to the lab is tormented. They are examined and tested for a week or two then a few are dissected for further study. In the back-left corner of the lab, there is a door that leads to a room where the other pixies are kept."

"How many Pixies are there?" questioned Tara.

"About a dozen."

"Murder!" shouted Tara ready to throw the cage that Kathleen was in against the far wall. Ralph stopped her saying, "Don't stoop to her level. What do pixies do when one breaks the law?"

"They are forced to wear a forest green with white trim jumpsuit while they serve the other pixies."

"Call Emma and tell her that we have a bad pixie for her to transport to the Pixie community."

Tisha reached in her purse, took out a green and white jumpsuit and asked, "Will this do?"

"It's perfect," stated Tara. She then gave it to Kathleen to put on.

Kathleen got Ralph's attention and stated, "Can I live here with you and Tara? I promise I will behave."

"You have two choices. Live at the lab, or with the pixies."

Peppy stated, "We can always let her go in the woods so she can fend for herself. But, with no wings, she wouldn't last a day."

Kathleen hung her head and said, "I'll live with the pixies."

Frank wandered into the basement with his hand on his head asking, "Kathleen, where are you?"

Ralph grabbed him by his collar and asked, "Shall we sentence him to the same fate?"

"What are you guys talking about and what did you do with Kathleen?"

Tara showed Frank his tiny friend, she then ordered, "As temporary head of the sprites, Frank is to be shrunk, then live the rest of his life serving other Pixies."

Frank stared at the small Kathleen and hollered, "What did you do to her?"

Ralph picked up Kathleen's tea cup and said, "Relax, no one is going to hurt you. Here is some nice cold Cinnamon Tea to help make all your problems small ones."

Frank finished the tea and began to feel lightheaded and in seconds he was only twelve inches tall. Peppy handed him some clothes, Tara put him in Kathleen's cage with a wire mesh divider. Frank held the metal bars of the cage and said, "I know in a few hours I will be big again."

"Not this time." stated Tara, "I will hand you to the pixie authorities for sentencing."

"For what?" harassing insects? I don't think so."

"Look around you Bug Nuggets, you have been permanently shrunk."

Frank turned to Kathleen and said, "I told you this was going to happen but no you had to listen to that jerk, Lester. Now, look where we are about to be scraped off the bottom of somebody's shoe."

Ralph asked, "Tara where do we bring these two?"

"I was going to call Emma and ask her but I think we should bring them to Little Ireland ourselves. Missy, I want you to guard the home while Ralph and I are away. Peppy; I think you should come along. You need some R and R back home."

Tisha questioned, "Would it be alright if I came too?"

"The more the merrier.

In Ralph's car, Tisha put a small sheet over Kathleen and Frank's cage, Tara, stated, "There is a small old pristine town, we go north and cross a river, then after three tenth of a mile; you will come to a dark stone bridge; turned right onto a narrow country road. That road will lead up a hill, through a meadow with a huge shade tree on the left. The road will end there and you need to continue on the dirt road which will circle around a crystal-clear lake. When you see a mountain with blue and light-yellow flowers rising out of the water. Park the car because we walk from there."

Tara stepped out of the car, handed the cage to Tisha, Peppy sat on Ralph's shoulder and Tara pointed and said, "We followed that narrow path until we came to a small village. Don't worry the people in the village are friendly with an attitude why do we have to go anywhere when everything we need is right here."

At the village, a young man greeted them with a warm smile and asked "How was your trip? Present, I hope." He gazed at Tara bowed and said, "Barefoot Princess the cave is through those woods to your right. But, I do have to ask you what do you have under the cloth?"

Tara showed the man Kathleen and Frank and said, "It's judgment time for them."

"I take it that's why you shrunk them."

"Pretty much."

Inside the cave, Tara pushed a rock on the cave wall that opened a passageway to a hidden valley.

In the passageway, Tara sneezed three times, gave Ralph and Tisha some pixie clothes then had them drink some cinnamon tea.

With the group, twelve inches tall, Tara opened the cage, tied a rope around Kathleen and Frank and led everyone into the hidden valley where they were immediately surrounded by three dozen male Pixies clad in green, pointing crossbows at them.

The leader ordered, "State your business! Oh, sorry Barefoot Princess welcome back."

Chapter 15

LITTLE IRELAND

Outside the lockup, Ralph scanned the high cliff laden with trees and the humble wooden homes with thatched roofs and said, "I can see why no one can find this place. It is vertically hidden from view."

After Frank and Kathleen were turned over to the Pixie Police, Peppy brought Tisha, Tara and Ralph to her parents' home. Two middle-aged Pixies opened the door, Peppy's father. Vic was a stout man with a white beard. Peppy's mom. Bess was a tall thin pixie with deep brown curly hair. They threw their arms around their daughter cried, "We were so worried that a human had killed you."

Bess stared at Peppy's wings and inquired, "What happened to your wings? They're not yours."

A human cut them off but I was given a wing graft. Thanks to my human friend Ralph."

Bess gazed at Tisha and Ralph and said, "Welcome to Little Ireland. I guess you can't stand outside, come in, come in and tell us all about yourselves. Ralph, how did you mate with the princess?"

In the living room that was made from odds and ends, Tisha sat on the couch, and Ralph sat on a chair made from a thimble and stated, "I met Tara by accident. I was in a garden waiting for a lady friend when I stepped in Tara's flight path. She glanced off my shoulder and landed in the flowerbed. I took her home and nursed her back to health."

An excited Tara piped up saying, "You should see his basement, Mrs. Bess. He turned it into a small replica of Little Ireland."

That evening Peppy's mom showed Tisha, Tara and Ralph their bedroom saying, "It's not often we have the Barefoot Princess and her mate stay oversight in our homes. See you guys in the morning. Oh, breakfast is at seven sharp."

In the room, Ralph looked at Tara and asked, "Now, what do we do? We can't sleep together we're not married."

Tara pulled back the covers and said, "We get ready for bed. You see when a pixie chooses a mate they hold hands the way we have been doing. So, Bess thinks that we plan to marry, that's why she put us in the same room."

"In other words, in your culture, we are married."

"Not exactly, but we are allowed to fool around until that day. However, tomorrow we have to get ready for the wedding the next day. Now, let's get ready for bed."

A stunned Ralph asked, "You mean with a pastor and everything?"

"Yes," stated Tara undoing the belt to her dress.

"What do I do? I don't have my Pjs with me."

Tara took off her dress saying, "So what. I sleep in the raw myself. Enough chit-chat, let's get in bed."

The next morning Ralph woke, lying on his back with Tara snuggled up to his side. He gently pulled back the covers, put one leg out when Tara grabbed him saying, "Oh no you don't, Mister it's only five in the morning and I am feeling kittenish. So, let's assume the lover's position because I've already taken off your undies."

"We are not married, so no fooling around." and rolled on his left side.

Tara snuggled against Ralph's back, put her arms around him, and began to kiss his neck. Ralph rolled over, looked at the excited expression on Tara's face and said, "Alright, I will show you how much I love you this morning. Do you wanna kiss?"

An hour and a half later, Ralph opened his eyes to see a chipper Tara lying next to him smiling, he inquired, "What?"

"Thank you for a lovely morning. Hey, we have a shower in our room, you want to join me? I need someone to wash my wings."

"No, you can have your shower first, I'm bushed."

"Oh, come on. Don't be a party pooper."

"Okay, lead the way. Oh, and could you wash my back when we are in there?"

Later, a dressed Ralph sat on the bed, looked at Tara in a forest green dress and patted the bed. She sat next to him and asked, "What is it, Sweetheart?"

"No matter what the culture of the county says, what we did this morning was wrong according to the Word of God and you know it."

Tara hugged her head and said, "Sorry Hon. I got so carried away with all the excitement of being in my home town again that I forgot."

"I forgive you now, let's pray."

At the breakfast table, Bess stated with a smile, "I trust you two got some sleep last night. This morning we have apple cinnamon oatmeal. Oh, Tara, the ladies of the town want to help you get ready for your wedding tomorrow. Mr. Ralph, you have to take your loving bride for the marriage license today.

At the bachelor party, a young female pixie clad in a thin hot pink dress sat next to Ralph and said, "Hi. I'm Kinkie, that is spelled K-I-N-K-I e. Are you a for real human?"

"Sure am."

"Wow, you look just like us without the wings, Kinkie pushed Ralph forward to study his back, she then asked, "Can I kiss you?"

"I guess that would be alright,"

Kinkie planted a wet kiss on Ralph's lips, giggled and said, "I don't believe I just kissed a human. Gotta go." She then gave him another kiss briskly rubbed his right arm and left.

At the wedding reception the next day, Ralph was dressed in a forest green tuxedo and Tara had on a lacy royal blue wedding dress that almost touched the floor. Ralph leaned over and asked Tara, "How come I am still small?"

"The food you are eating is keeping you the proper size. Don't worry you will be big again."

A slender male pixie dressed in a blue pinstriped suit sat next to Ralph, handed him a piece of paper with names on it and said, "This is a list of pixies that are missing from our community. Please do your best to find them."

A commotion quickly caught Ralph's attention he walked to the elderly woman hollering at Peppy. Held up his hand saying, "Please settle down. Now, what's the problem?"

The woman pointed to Peppy's wings and stated, "She stole my daughter Beebe's wings!"

"No, she didn't. I found those wings hanging on a human's wall as a trophy. Peppy's were cut off and they were grafted onto Peppy. I am so sorry ma'am. But, that may mean only one thing."

The Pixie began to cry, Peppy held her arm saying, "Can you tell me about your daughter?"

The Pixie paused, looked at Ralph and said, "Promise me that you will find the ones who killed my Beebe, and make them pay."

"Yes ma'am, I will."

Right after the reception, Ralph took Tara to the town lockup and asked, "We would like to see the human prisoners."

The guard brought them to a sturdy transparent plastic wall. Ralph walked up to it Kathleen and asked, "What's been happening? You look nice."

"Are they treating you well?"

"Oh yes, I have my own apartment with a high fenced in backyard. I cook meals, and mend clothing for the Pixies of the community." Kathleen fell to her knees and cried, "I was so wrong to do what I did. Please forgive me?"

"How is Frank doing?"

"He has the place next to mine and has to do laundry for a lot of Pixies."

"I forgive you. Oh, Tara and I were just married today."

Kathleen tightened her fist, her face darkened and screamed, "You what?"

"Tara and I were married today."

Kathleen pounded on the plastic wall screaming, "If I get my hand on you so help me I will kill you both!"

The guard tapped Ralph's shoulder saying, "You are gonna have to leave."

"One more minute." Ralph showed Kathleen the list of missing pixies and pleaded, "Kathleen, you know what happened to these missing pixies for the love of God tell me."

Kathleen squared her shoulders looked Ralph in his eyes, and stated, "Why don't you go to," just then a sedative dart struck Kathleen's shoulder, her eyes rolled back in her head as she collapsed on the floor.

Ralph turned to the guard and said, "They may not have wings like you, but they are very dangerous."

That night, Tara snuggled up to Ralph in bed and said, "I have to admit, being with you like this after the wedding feels a whole lot better."

"No guilt feelings when you are married,"

"You got that right,"

"In the morning. You want the shower first."

"Nope. We shower together. Remember you have to wash my wings and I have to scrub your back. Besides, we have to save water."

"No arguments here."

In the morning, Tara opened her eyes to find Ralph huddled on the very edge of the bed, and she asked, "Why are you way over on your side of the bed? Are you mad at me?"

"You scared the crap out of me last night. I woke up about two thirty in the morning to a loud buzzing sound. I thought a bunch of bees had gotten under our bed and was terrified of getting stung."

"That was me. I have a bad habit of buzzing my wings in my sleep Sorry. Now come here husband of mine so I can give you a back rub."

"Do you know that I had the chance to sleep with Mrs. Walters last night."

"Where is that shameless hussy? I'll rip her wings off and stuff them down her throat!" screamed Tara.

"You're Mrs. Walters silly."

"Ah, yeah, I knew that. Hey, why don't I take you to the water slide? It will be loads of fun."

"Unfortunately, I don't have any money."

"Don't worry,, it only cost two bugs and a butterfly."

"You people carry dead insects around in your pocket? That is gross. I am not going to keep A bunch bugs in my pocket. No way."

"Relax. That's the Pixies way of saying that it is free."

"OK, then, let's go as long as we can get a bathing suit there."

Walking across town hand in hand with Tara, Ralph stated, "I'm surprised to see that the sprites here have police, fire, military and a social structure that is just like the humans."

"What did you expect a bunch of half-naked pixie running around with no order?"

"You're right that was stupid of me to say that, I'm sorry."

Tara stopped in front a hill some five stories high. Pointed to a blue water slide that wound around boulders and trees. Ralph stared with his mouth opened in shock, "That's a suicide slide."

"You can always use the kids slide if you're too scared."

Ralph put on his bathing suit, paused at the top of the slide, grab a pad took a deep breath and went for it.

Somewhere around 2/3 of the way down the water slide it took a sharp 90° turn to the left. Ralph was going too fast to make the turn and went over the top of the slide and scraped his back. The Pixies in charge of medical emergency were on the scene in seconds. Paramedic Betty rolled Ralph on his stomach to tend to his in injuries and thought, "Oh no, his wings are gone. She then shouted, "Larry. We have a code one. See what you can do to find this guy's wings!" She then reassured him, "Don't worry. you're going to be all right will find your wings right now I want you to lie down and be still."

Ralph stated, "Just give me something for the scrapes on my back and I'll be on my way, honest I'm fine."

"You can't walk around without your wings now lie down."

"I don't have wings, I'm a human. Now, give me something for my back."

Betty cried, "Eeeeeewwwwwww! I touched a human without protection! I'm gonna die of some horrible disease, somebody please help!"

Tara flew to Ralph's side, and stated, "Betty, all those stories you've heard about humans being disease carriers are just stories, I should know, I'm married to that human."

Within minutes the pixie hazmat team were on the scene spraying Ralph with green foam. Tara tried to explain to them that he wasn't a threat to anyone but, they would not listen to her."

In the medical center's isolation ward, Ralph lay on his bunk in a white jumpsuit trying to figure out how to explain to them that he was not a medical hazard.

The next day, Tara walked down the hall of the medical center, tapped on the window where Ralph was and waved to him. He put his hand on the glass, Tara put her hand on his saying. "I miss you. I am sorry they would not let me in to see you until now." Tara approached the doctor and inquired, "When are you going to release my husband?"

"When I know he isn't a threat to our society."

Just then a nurse put a manila folder on the doctor's desk, he read the report then said. "Wait a minute ma'am. The tests we did on your husband are all negative so he is free to go, just sign this release form."

Dressed in his normal clothes, Ralph walked up to the doctor and inquired, "Could I see the lady sprite in the next room?"

"I don't know we're getting her ready to be transferred to Sunny Acres Sanatorium."

"In other words, 'the funny farm.'" stated Tara.

Ralph stated, "I have to see her."

"Alright you two can go in, but you do so at your own risk."

Ralph and Tara slowly entered a dark room that had a single bed and a window with the shade pulled down. In the far-left corner sat a female Pixie on the floor dressed in a white jumpsuit with her head down. Her arms were folded across her chest and she was rocking back and forth. Ralph sat on the floor in front of the sprite with Tara by his side, and he asked, "The other day I heard you say something about a laboratory. Did you mean Specialty Labs?"

The Pixie stared at the floor as she said, "Go away."

Ralph inquired, "Was Stan the one who performed some tested on you?"

The Pixie jerked her head up and silently started at Ralph.

Tara asked, "Were there other Pixies in the lab besides you?"

The Pixie nodded her head yes.

"What did they do to you that was so horrible?"

The Pixie just shook her head no.

Ralph inquired, "Did you hear the cries of another Pixie being teased and that's what terrified you and was that Pixie's name, Peppy?"

Tears whelmed up in the pixie's eyes as she fell into Ralph's arms and cried for five minutes.

Ralph held her saying, "No one is going to hurt you, that I promise."

The Pixie dried her eyes and asked. "You believe me?"

"Yes, because my wife and I rescued a Pixie by the name of Peppy from that very same lab."

"Please forgive my lack of manners, I am Susan, I was captured and brought there three a week before Peppy." choked with emotions, Susan put her head down and said, "The screams of anguish I heard from the other pixies being teased sent cold chills up my back. Each night I tried to go to sleep wondering if I was going to be next. But a young lady with short, blond hair, gave me a few pieces of cloth to wear and she was the reason why I stayed alive. Because every time Stan came for me, she would tell him that I was very sick. Peppy was screaming and hollering something fierce the day they brought her in. I could not see much because my cage was on the other side of the lab, but I heard one human say, shut up and Peppy let go a scream and then nothing. The torment they put that poor thing through was monstrous."

Tara stated, "Peppy escaped and is back in Little Ireland." Tara assisted Susan to stand and asked, "Would you like to go for a walk?"

"Sure."

Chapter 16

RALPH'S DOUBT

Outside the hospital, Tara took her husband to a restaurant called 'Flynn's'. Ralph examined the craftsmanship of the leather seats and the gold curlicue carvings on the walls and stated, "It is hard to believe that you Pixies can do such fantastic carpentry."

"Hon. You're doing it again."

"Doing what?"

"You are letting your ignorance show."

A stout, male pixie walked up to Ralph, glanced at his back, shook his hand and explained, "I take it you are human. I'm the manager and I could not help over hearing your statement about the craftsmanship of the buildings in Little Ireland. Just because we are small doesn't mean we live off the humans' cast offs. True, a side of beef will feed us Pixies for quite a long time. But, check out the detail in that hand carved statue of our mayor or the needlework on that tapestry hanging on that wall over there."

"You people are truly underestimated."

Sitting in a booth, with a wooden table Ralph stated, "I am glad they released Susan from the hospital and that she is going to help us to shut down that lab." Ralph smiled and stated, "I suppose the Pixies here have small hens that lay tiny eggs."

Tara frowned and stated, "Ralph, really, don't be so stupid."

"Sorry. How about we order. I am having an omelet with home fries. What about you Sweet?"

"I'll have a short stack of strawberry pancakes."

When the waitress served the food, Ralph stared at his omelet and home fries and stated, "There isn't a difference between this food and what I get in the local diner back home. I know, I know I'm being insensitive again. I guess I'll have a big slice of humble pie for dessert."

The next day, Ralph talked to the Mayor of the city and stated, "If I were you I would put a ban on traveling to the human world until the men who are committing the atrocities on the pixies are caught and punished."

The mayor stared at Ralph and said, "If I do that a lot of the commerce we depend on outside this valley will suffer greatly."

"What's more important? The lives of the people in the community or the money in your pocket?"

"I have heard the stories of Pixies being caught and brutalized but I am not sure that they are true."

"Then ask Susan and Peppy. They were in the human lab and escaped."

"Look human. Pixies are agile and fast which makes it virtually impossible for a human to catch them. So, how can a human apprehend a pixie?"

"How indeed."

"Good day to you, Ralph."

At Bess and Vic's home, Tara asked Peppy, "How did the labs catch you?"

"I was told to go to a large field of flowers; just north of the lab. While I was laying on a sunflower catching some rays, I heard a high-pitched sound that knocked me out, the next thing I knew I am in a cage in the buff."

Vic explained, "As you know Tara, pixies can't be picked up by radar, or any scanning device. However, a long-range motion sensor can be set to detect a sprite if the high range amplifier is hooked up just right. I hate to say this but only pixies know to do this."

Ralph stated, "That means the pixie motion sensor has to be hooked up to a high-end amplifier that will render the pixie unconscious."

"Is there a certain color flower that will captivate a pixie?"

"Bright reds, blues, and yellows will definitely attract a pixie." stated Vic.

"That's what the field had in it," stated Peppy.

Ralph stated, "Then there has to be a snitch in Little Ireland, especially if Kathleen and her cohorts knew that there is such a thing as a pixie druggist."

"Which means he or she is living high on the hog." stated Tara, "Alright everyone here is your assignment. Find the fink that is selling the Pixies for financial gain."

Ralph stared at Peppy and asked, "Are you alright? You seem to be breathing funny."

"I am fine, honest."

"Tara, take Peppy in the kitchen, get her clothes off, then put her on the table so I can give her an exam."

"Do you know what you are doing?"

"I used to be a Physician's Assistant."

In the kitchen, an embarrassed, red-faced Peppy, lie on the kitchen table, stared at Ralph, smiled, and said, "You just wanted a peek at me naked."

Ralph asked, "Can your roll on your stomach?" He then asked, "Where did you get these scratches on your back?"

"I went to see Kathleen today and the guard let me in her cell. After we talked for a minute or two, she hit me, I fell back and a whole bunch of stuff that landed on top of me. But, she apologized when the guard came in to help me up."

Peppy rolled on her back, held out her arms to Ralph and said, "Come here and give me a hug."

"Can the cute talk, and tell me where you got that big bruise just below your left breast?"

"I got them when all that stuff fell on me and it is a little sore too."

Ralph pressed on Peppy's pelvic area saying, "Does it hurt when I press here?"

"Yes, that hurts big time."

Ralph placed his hand high up on Peppy's inner thigh and inquired, "How did you get these bruises? Was some boy trying to get fresh with you?"

"I know, I know I shouldn't have done it but I went in Frank's cell to talk to him first. He got too friendly with me and the guard had to knock him out in order to get him off me. That's when I visited Kathleen. Boy, was that ever a mistake."

"I have to ask you this. Did Frank, you know?"

"He didn't even come close to doing it. He ah, grabbed me there."

"Get dressed and have your parents take you to the emergency room so a doctor can check you over."

"Am I gonna die?"

"No. you are just badly banged up, now how about that hug?"

Peppy dressed, went to her father and asked, "Dad, I am sorry for my rebellious attitude. Can you lead me to Christ?"

Vic hollered, "Bess, come here. Our daughter wants to come home to the Lord."

At the lockup, Ralph approached the guard and said, "Why don't you take a break but leave the keys on your desk?"

With the guard gone, Ralph unlocked Frank's cell walked in, looked him in the eye and asked, "I hear you had a cute female visitor?"

Frank smiled, but before he could make a comment, Ralph landed a hard-right cross to his jaw sending him to the floor. Then stated, "Don't even think of touching Peppy again!"

Ralph entered Kathleen's cell, locked the door behind him and said, "Peppy is a young pixie, why did you hit her?"

"It was an accident."

Ralph's hand shot out, grabbed Kathleen by her throat, squeezed and asked, "Who told you how to capture a pixie and how did you know that there was such a thing as a pixie druggist?"

Kathleen gasped for air, as she stated, "I don't know what you are talking about."

"Yes, you do know. Because humans don't have the slightest idea how to capture a Pixie because they are only a myth to them." Ralph threw Kathleen against the transparent wall saying, "I am not leaving here until you tell me who gave you the information."

Kathleen staggered to her feet and asked, "Sweetheart, why are you doing this to me? Don't you know how much I love you?"

Ralph belted Kathleen in her stomach, knocking the wind out of her. She bent over gasping for air and whispered, "His name is Ben the Carpenter."

Ralph grabbed Kathleen by her shoulders, slammed her against the transparent wall, got in her face and said, "The next time you hurt another pixie so help me I will twist that lovely head right of yours off your neck." Ralph let Kathleen collapse on the floor, left the cell, and threw the keys back on the desk.

When the guard returned, Kathleen stuck her head in the visitor's window in the clear wall and hollered, "Guard! Are you going to just sit there and let him get away with what he did to me?"

"I didn't see or hear a thing, now get away from that opening and quiet down."

"He just tried to kill me! Do something!"

The guard picked up his crossbow, pointed it at Kathleen's head, saying, "You have three seconds to step away from the window before I shoot."

Ralph placed his hand on the guard's arm saying, "Allow me." he approached Kathleen, who was hollering all kinds of accusations at him. Hauled off and belted her in the face, sending her to the floor out cold. Turned to the guard and said, "Some people have to learn the hard way. Good day to you."

Walking home, Ralph stopped in a diner, sat on a stool at the counter. A short pixie waitress with blond hair asked, "Hey, Doll Face what will you have?"

"Just water."

"Hey, you are that human everyone is talking about. Whatever you want is on me."

Ralph looked at her name tag and said, "Madelyn. Give me coffee, and a burger."

"Coming right up." The waitress then asked, "Why so down in the mouth?"

"A few minutes ago, I lost my temper and kicked the crap out of a woman."

"Can I ask you why?"

"Her boyfriend got fresh with a young female Pixie and his girlfriend almost killed her. I mean she is barely 22 years old, never hurt a soul and didn't deserve to be treated like that."

"This pixie. that was knocked around so much. Was it Peppy?"

"The very same."

"Yeah, her father comes in here all the time. How is she doing?"

"Her parents just took her to the hospital with scrapes and bruises all over her body."

"Not to change the subject, but is it true that humans are catching pixies to experiment on?"

"Yes. Susan and Peppy were fortunate to escape from their lab. Peppy had her wings cut off. But had a wing graft that was successful."

The waitress held out her hand saying, "I get off work in an hour. You wanna walk down the street holding hands."

"You are asking me if I want to fool around with you. Sorry, I am married to Tara."

"The barefoot Princess?"

"That's her."

"Then you must be a Duke. Wow, I just served royalty."

"Humans have a way to show respect to women." Ralph held pixie Madelyn's hand and kissed the back of it."

She stared at the back of her hand and said, "I like that custom. It gave me goose pimples."

"Thank you for the meal but I have to go."

"Ralph, before you go. What brought you to Little Ireland?"

"To stop the violent death of Pixies by humans."

An elderly male pixie sat on a stool next to Ralph, and said, "Son. It is imperative that you stop the humans from catching us Pixies because sooner or later they will find our valley. When that happens, our way of life will vanish forever and we will become vagabonds, living in the trash heaps of the world."

"Two of the humans are already in custody and are held in the lockup here in this valley. But, I have to locate a snitch called Ben the Carpenter."

"I don't know him but I am sure that you will find him."

"But what surprises me. Why hasn't Ben told the humans where Little Ireland is located."

"That's because if he does, the humans will stop paying him and his life of ease will come to an end."

"So, any Pixie that is living in the lap of luxury I should check out."

"Exactly! I'll talk to you later, son."

When Ralph left the diner, the shadows on the mountain side said that it would soon be dark soon. Still feeling upset over how he lost his temper with Frank and how he abused Kathleen, he wandered in a nearby park. Found a tree away from the street light, sat down to wrestle with the pain and confusion inside him. Ralph knew that his answer was in Christ, but he had to struggle for his recovery that would come through patience.

Ralph smiled as he remembered when he first met Kathleen, how sweet and kind she was. When Ralph pondered about her tender touch and warm embrace he wondered if he was right in marrying Tara. After all, a marriage to a pixie would not be legal in a court of law and he could easily dumped Tara and marry Kathleen.

Ralph was about to get up and go back to the lockup and ask Kathleen if she would take him back. When he felt the warm and tender touch of a pixie woman's hand. The gentle fragrance of her perfume told Ralph that it was Tara. She sat next to him and asked. "There you are. Is there anything I can do to help you through your pain?"

"How did you find me?"

"It's not hard to find a human in a city full of pixies. Now, what's bothering you?"

"I beat the crap out of Kathleen today."

"If you wouldn't have, I would of."

"You don't understand, men do not hit women, especially Christian men. This afternoon I came short of killing Kathleen. I was in love with her and was going to spend the rest of my life with that woman."

"Do you regret marrying me?"

"Right now, my mind is crowded with thoughts and I can't answer you."

Tara snuggled up to Ralph saying, "I'm gonna stay here with you and see you through your trouble."

Chapter 17

A STICKY SITUATION

The next morning in the park, Ralph opened his eyes, saw Tara nestled against his side, and realized how much she was devoted to him.

Tara opened her eyes, looked at Ralph and said, "You look surprised that I'm still here."

"Kathleen was never the one to stick around when I had a problem and no I don't regret marrying you." Ralph went to stand and moaned, "I shouldn't have slept against that tree, my back is killing me."

"Take off your shirt, loosen your pants, then lie down on your stomach so I can give you a back rub."

While Tara was massaging the small of Ralph's back she questioned, "Were you a real P-A, or was that just an excuse get a peek at Peppy?"

"I did work in a doctor's office, giving people physical exams. Ah, Tara Sweet, you're getting too low with your message."

"It's too early in the morning for someone to come by and see what I am doing. Do you know that you have a red mark on your tush? Hon, one more thing. Why did you give Peppy a hug when she wasn't dressed? That was unprofessional and it could have led to something else."

Ralph stated in defense, "Come on Tara you know I wouldn't cheat on you especially when you are right there watching. Are you finished with the back rub? Because I don't want someone coming by and see me like this?"

"It's our honeymoon and I want to have some memorable fun. You wanna sneak one in the park?"

Ralph lie on his back with his eyes closed saying, "All I want to do is lay here and relax before we go home." he reached behind him, touched his wife's hip as she snuggled up to him, he opened his eyes and asked, "What are you doing?"

"There is a large bush over there. Shall we go inside it and sneak one in the park?"

"Okay, come on. I just hope no one sees us."

An hour and twenty minutes later, Ralph poked his head out of the bush, whispered, "The coast is clear." he then walked out of the large shrub with his shirt on his shoulder.

Tara stopped, and asked, "Hon, can you zip up the back of my dress?"

"Just a minute, you have bits of twig and junk stuck to your back from where you were lying on the ground. Okay, you're good to go."

Tara spun around, with a smile on her face, threw her arms around Ralph, and said, "Admit it. you enjoyed it."

"I don't believe I let you talk me into it."

Tara placed her head on Ralph's bare chest and said, "I wish you would learn to relax."

"The next time we sneak one in the park I think we should bring a beach towel to lie on."

"Then you did enjoy fooling around."

"Of course, I did. I'm just not used to doing things like that outside. Oh, before we go, let me check the back of your head for stuff. The last thing you need to do is advertise what we were doing."

Ralph held Tara's hand saying, "Let's go see what they are doing at the park stage."

The male Pixie stood in the center of the stage, hollered "Turn the emitters on and a line all five of them so they are pointing at the center of the stage. Good! Now activate the 3D singer program."

A three-dimensional image of a male vocalist appeared on stage and began to sing, 'My Country Home.'" The Pixie then stated, "Good. Now turn up the volume! Excellent okay, lock the settings."

Ralph turned to his wife and asked, "Since when did Pixies have 3-D imaging? We humans don't even have that technology."

"We Pixies have lots of things that you humans don't have. You wanna come to the concert tomorrow night?"

"I wouldn't miss it for the world." Hey, there is a diner close by why don't we grab breakfast, and plan our next move."

In the diner enjoying their breakfast, Ralph stated, "Kathleen told me that Ben the Carpenter has been feeding information to the humans."

"How are we going to find one Pixie in a valley this size?

"All we have to do is find the town's registry and look up the Bens."

"The police chief entered the diner, sat next to him and stated, "I don't know about where you live human, but in this valley, one does not walk in a lockup and beat the snot out of a prisoner. Now, she wants to file a complaint against you."

"A complaint? Do you know how badly Kathleen and Frank hurt Peppy?"

"She told me that it was an accident."

"Chief. Get your fact straight before you start accusing people. It was no accident that Frank molested Peppy when she went to talk to him, and it was no accident that Kathleen hit Peppy so hard that it threw her into a pile of junk that fell on top of her. Ask your guards they will tell you. Kathleen and Frank are dangerous criminals and the guard should not have allowed Peppy in their cell. Which means chief, this whole thing falls on your head."

"Well ah, maybe I was a bit too hasty in my judgment. I'll talk to my superior about the two humans."

"You do that."

When the chief left, the waitress walked up to Ralph, handed him a thick book saying, "Someone left this for you."

Tara glanced at the book and said, "It's the town registry. Thank you."

Back at Bess and Vic's place, Bess handed Ralph the doctor prescription for Peppy's bruises.

Ralph read the prescription, rub pineapples on the bruises to promote healing because it is a good anti-inflammatory and will help reduce any swelling associated with bruising. Cold tea can also be used because it contains tannins that constrict blood vessels. You can apply black tea or green tea directly to the bruised area which will reduce discoloration.

Bess then stated, "The doctor told me that he wanted you to do the treatments because you know what to do."

"I will need a large amount of black tea for Peppy to bathe in. Can you do that?"

"I'll get my friends to help."

Tisha stated, "I saw a sale of tea a few blocks from here. Be back in a few minutes.

Five hours later, the bathtub in the large main bathroom was half full of black tea. Bess flipped a switch on the wall saying, "I turned on the warming element under the tub so the tea doesn't get cold."

When Peppy removed her bathrobe, Ralph noticed that most of her body was now black and blue, and asked, "Are you okay?"

"Oh yeah, big time."

Tara placed a bath towel on the toilet and assisted Peppy in the tub saying, "Scrunch down until only your head is above the tea."

"How long do I have to be in here?"

Ralph answered, "You will need three, twenty-minute treatments a day until the black and blue goes away."

Peppy locked her eyes on Ralph and asked, "Could you stay in here with me?"

"I guess so."

Tara stated, "I'll start searching the town registry for Ben." and left.

Feeling uneasy about being in the bathroom alone with Peppy when she was soaking in the tub. Ralph asked, "How many beaus do you have?"

"None right now. because all they want to do is massage my hand with their thumb while they hold it."

"In other words, they wanted to get into it with you. As a concerned friend, have you ever allowed a boy to talk you into doing it with him?"

"If you mean have I ever mated with a boy? I am embarrassed to say that there was this one time that it almost happened. But, I am so glad that daddy didn't find out or he would have ripped his wings off for sure."

"Do you want to talk about it?"

"Please don't say a word to anyone about what I am going to tell you."

"You have my word."

"Two years ago, I was naive concerning all the mating practices. A cute boy came up to me in the park, held my hand and began to rub it with his thumb. When we came to a large bush next to a tree, he brought me inside and I was shocked when he immediately divested himself of his clothes. Before I knew what was going on, he was trying to mate with me. A police officer hollered, "What's going on inside that bush?"

"I grabbed my clothes, flew straight up in the air and hid in a cloud so I could dress. The boy was arrested for nudity and I never saw him again. Other boys approached me but I turned them away because of the part of my body they were staring at."

"I suppose you felt used when the boy tried to force himself on you."

"Big time and I cringe every time I think about how stupid I was back then."

"Try casting that time of embarrassment on the Lord for He cares for you."

"I am so used to doing things myself that I never thought about asking the Lord for help."

"I think you soaked in the tea long enough, come on out."

Peppy stood holding her back and asked, "Before you dry my wings, could you massage the lower part of my back? It hurts something fierce."

Ralph stood, helped Peppy out of the tub, handed her a towel, sat on the toilet, and had Peppy stand between his knees. He then rubbed the small of her back with his thumbs for a good five minutes, before he let his hands slip down to her bare butt. A few minutes later, Peppy turned around with a broad smile on her face. Ralph was about to give her a long passionate kiss when Tara hollered from the other side of the bathroom door, "Is everything alright in there?"

Peppy quickly wrapped the towel around her, opened the bathroom door and left.

Tara stared at her husband and stated, "Will you forgive me? That was unfair of me to leave you alone in the bathroom with Peppy. The last thing you need right now is to have that kind of pressure on you."

Feeling guilty, Ralph stated, "Nothing happened between us. But, when she has to have her next treatment in four hours I want you to be in there monitoring her, not me."

Tara felt the dampness on her husband's hands and asked, "Did you like rubbing Peppy's tushy."

"Yes, ah no. Sorry."

Tara entered the bathroom, closed the door, stepped out of her dress said to Ralph, "Let me help you forget about Peppy."

Forty-five minutes later, Ralph opened the bathroom door smiling, and tucking his shirt inside his pants.

Tara left the bathroom fixing her dress and stated, "I have gone through seventy pages of the town registry and have not found a Ben the Carpenter anywhere. If you will excuse me I am going to our bedroom to lie down and rest my eyes. Call me when it is time for Peppy's next treatment."

Ralph sat at a table in the den and began to read the list of names, when Peppy sat next to him clad in shorts and a halter top and said, "From the first time I lead eyes on you, I wanted to get you alone. Tara doesn't know about the number of time I snuck into your room and watched you shower. Then when you had to watch me in the bathroom I saw my chance to get you to notice me." Peppy hung her head and said, "But, when you began to rub my bare butt I wanted more."

Ralph stared at Peppy and said, "Now you know what you wanted to do with me was wrong."

"Yes, and I am sorry for coming on to you the way I did. Oh, can I tell you one more thing? I lied to you about the boy in the park. I was trying to show you that I am a mature Pixie and could handle myself when we mate. Please forgive me. Would you mind if I had Tara watch me during my next treatment? Because I don't want to get tangled up in the mess I just repented of."

"That's fine with me. If it is alright with you I have to give you the final exam to make sure you're OK."

"I'm good with that. Would you like me to fix you something to eat while you're going over the town registry?"

"Sure, I would like a tuna fish, with lettuce, tomato, and whip cream sandwich."

"Whip cream with tuna fish? That is so gross."

"I'm just put in your wings. A regular tuna fish sandwich would be great."

"By the way what are you looking for?"

"Tara and I are looking for a pixie by the name of Ben the Carpenter, have you heard of him?"

"I think he's the pixie that's been going around in the valley helping people financially. Is he the one responsible for me being caught by the lab?"

"It is a great possibility that he's been informing the humans who to catch and where."

"He doesn't look like the type that would sell his own kind for a few bucks."

"You can't judge a Pixie's heart by their action or how they are dressed."

"You've got that right. But, are you sure that Kathleen didn't give you a false lead just to get you off her back? After all, she is an excellent liar."

"Kathleen speaks the truth every now and then but to deliberately lie to me. No, I can't believe that about her."

"Kathleen did tell you that she stopped seeing Frank and posed as Miss Innocence when she was with you, but, was fooling around with Frank all along. What about all those back rubs she gave you? While she was acting like she cared about you, but actuality she was going to steal you blind then take off with Frank."

"I guess I should take my own advice."

Peppy smiled and said, "You got that right. Now, if you will excuse me I have to make you a snack."

Ten minutes later, Peppy put a plate down on the table with two sandwiches. Ralph put her in a headlock, and briskly rubbed his knuckles on her head. Peppy hollered, "Not the nuggies!"

Chapter 18

KATHLEEN ON THE LOOSE

Mid-afternoon the next day, Peppy had just finished her fifth tea treatment, walked out of the bathroom with Tara right behind trying to wrap a bark blue towel around her. Tara asked, "Hon, I don't think Peppy needs any more treatments. What do you think?"

"Bring Peppy in the den and let me take a look."

In the den with his wife, Ralph took off Peppy's bath towel, examined the faded black and blue marks and stated, "Looking good lady, however, your left butt cheek is red. Where you bitten on your tush by a deadly Brown Widow Spider?"

A nervous Peppy inquired, "I Don't think so. Why? Am I have to go to the hospital again?"

"Your whole left butt cheek is bright red which means it may have to be cut off."

Tara belted Ralph on his shoulder saying, "Will you stop scaring poor Peppy."

Peppy stated, "You mean I'm not going to be buttless."

"You may smell like tea for a couple of days but you are going to be fine. Now, get dressed, or do you want to run around feeling free."

Peppy gave Ralph a quick jab to his shoulder saying, "That's for scaring the pants off me."

Ralph tossed her towel to Peppy saying, "Put your towel back on!"

"Sorry. When Daddy is at work, I like to relax." and dropped the towel.

"But, I am here so please cover up."

Tara stared at Peppy perky figure as she took her sweet time wrapping the towel around her. She then eyes Ralph watching her and thought. "*This is not a health environment for my marriage. Peppy has the hots for Ralph for and is trying to entice him into doing something he shouldn't. So, it's time we found a new place.*" Tara then said, "Hon, we have to find another place to stay." She then nudged her husband saying, "Can you take your eyes off what Peppy is doing for at least a minute and listen to me."

"Oh, ah sorry what do you want Tushy, ah, I mean Hon."

"I want to talk to you, outside."

Out in the backyard, Tara lead, Ralph to large rock joined on three sides by a flower garden. Sat down with her husband and said, "I think it's time we found another place to live."

"What's wrong with living here?"

"Look, Sweetheart, Peppy is flirting with you and I am not going to stand around and watch you drooling all over her, every time she shakes that little butt of hers."

"I never noticeded Peppy was attracted to me."

"A woman knows when someone is after her mate, and if Peppy keeps coming on to you the way she has been. She will need another wing graft because I'm gonna rip them off, and shove them down her throat!"

"Where do you want to go?"

"I'd rather sleep in the park than risk the chance of losing you to Peppy."

"Okay pack your things and let's go."

Tara gave Bess a hug saying, "We have to be going."

"Where will you two stay?"

"We are not sure yet."

"My brother has a cabin on the north mountain, give me a minute to call him, prayerfully you two can stay there."

Five minutes later, Bess reported, "I've got great news. You and your husband can stay in my brother's cabin as long as you like."

"How do we get there?"

"When you leave the yard, turn right and walk to the coffee shop just up the street. Clint will meet you there."

Peppy slowly approached Tara with her head down and said, "I know it's my fault that you are leaving. Because I threw myself at your mate."

"No problem. Just keep your eyes on Christ."

Ralph and Tara entered a quaint coffee shop that had framed photos of famous Pixies all over the wall. They sat in a booth and ordered two coffees and burgers. A male Pixie in his fifties walked in clad in jeans, a red plaid shirt, and a beard. Greeted Ralph and Tara saying, "My sister told me that you wanted to use my cabin."

Ralph shook his hand saying, "Sit and have a cup. How much do you charge per month?"

"Two bugs and a butterfly. Oh, I'm Clint."

At the log cabin that had a nice front porch, Clint handed Ralph the key saying, "Just don't destroy the place. Later."

Ralph slowly opened the cabin door, nervous that he would find a disaster inside. Instead, he found a neat cabin with wooden rafters, a fire place made out of field stone, a wooden table by the window and a bedroom off to the left that had a feather bed. Tara inquired, "Where is the bathroom?"

Ralph opened the back door, pointed to a little house with a half-moon on the door and asked, "Is that what you are looking for?"

A shocked Tara said, "You have got to be kidding me, and that wooden stall fifty feet from the left side of the cabin I suppose is the shower."

"You guessed it."

"You mean I have to go outside with just a towel around me? No, not going to happen!"

"There is a walkway to the shower that has walls which means all they will see is your feet and head."

Tara stared at the wall and said, "Not much of a privacy wall if you ask me."

"Everything from your shoulders to your knees is hidden."

Tara stared at the walkway to the shower, then said, "You first. Go inside take everything off and walk to the shower. I'll watch and see if you are right."

Tara carefully studied Ralph's bare shoulders and knees all the way to the shower. When Ralph entered the stall, Tara peeked over that partition and said, "I think I can shower outside, as long as we don't have any visitors."

Ralph smiled and said, "I love it, the water is nice and warm."

"Hold that thought. I'm coming in with you."

In the shower, Tara rested her arms on Ralph's shoulders stated, "After we shower, I want to try out that feather bed with you."

Later, Ralph and Tara sat in two wicker chairs on the front porch, Ralph inquired, "So, tomorrow we check out this Ben character."

The next day right after breakfast, Tara stood behind Ralph outside, hooked her arms under his shoulders and took flight. Then lit down at the beginning of a dead-end street to check out the street vendors. While they were talking to an elderly Pixie woman, who was selling vegetables, Susan approached them and stated, "I forgot to tell you one important thing. I received a note from an unknown source telling me to go to the field of flowers just north of the lab. Then bring back some bright red and blues flowers for a hefty sum of money. That's when I was caught."

The woman selling vegetables stated, "My daughter received the same letter the other day. But she was in the middle of a business transaction and didn't go."

Ralph informed the street vendor, "If you know of anyone else that received a letter like that. Tell them that it is a trap." Ralph turned to Susan and asked, "Do you know who sent you the letter?"

"No, But the initial was 'S'. Hey, talk to you later, a social group wants me to give a talk about humans."

Late that afternoon, Ralph and Tara sat at a table in a sidewalk cafe. The Pixie waitress took their order and Ralph asked Tara, "Can I see that list of names you found in the registry?" Ralph checked off all the names saying, "We've talked to every Ben in the list. Now, what do we do and where does the 'S' fit in all this?"

A well dressed male Pixie sat down at their table looked at Ralph and stated, "Good afternoon, I'm Benjamin Carpenter. You two look like you could use some financial assistance."

"Actually, I am a human here trying to find somebody that will help me with my endeavor."

"Oh. What may that be?"

"I have a lab and I want to analyze some Pixie, preferably female. Would you know a Pixie that would help me? All you have to do is send me a few choices Pixies by sending them a letter telling them where to go and sweeten it by telling them that they would earn lots of cash."

"I suppose you are trying to lure this lovely pixie into your devious trap. Sir, I'm going to have you arrested."

Tara put her coffee down, and said, "That human is my husband and we are trying to find the Pixie that's been doing the same thing and Kathleen directed us to you."

"Are you talking about that useless piece of human flesh in the lockup? If you are, she lied to you."

Ralph inquired, "Would you know of a pixie that would stoop that low?"

"Yeah, Steven the Chief of police. He is the kind of so-and-so that would do something like that."

"I take it the Steven isn't well liked here in Little Ireland."

"He uses his badge to take advantage on females in lockup. Why I wouldn't be surprised he has mated with that human female."

"Thank you, Benjamin. My wife and I will check him out as soon as possible."

"Is there anything I can do to help?"

Ralph handed Benjamin the list of missing Pixies and said, "A lot of families are going to be heartbroken when they get the news that their loved ones were mutilated to death."

"I'll round up my friends to setup a Relief found. Gotta go."

Ralph stared at the tree near by them asked his wife, "Did you see something move in that tree?"

"You're seeing things. Let's go back home and regroup. I want to nab this Pixie lowlife so bad it isn't even funny."

Walking up the mountain path to the cabin, a Pixie all decked out in forest green garb swooped down and tackled Ralph and Tara to the ground. Ralph stared at Peppy's green outfit and face, asked, "What's the big idea knocking us off our feet?"

Peppy pointed to a tree with six arrows sticking in it and said, "Another second longer and you two would have in tomorrow's obituary."

"Why the green outfit?"

Peppy smiled and said, "I am the Green Shadow that's been helping the police."

Tara gave Peppy a hug saying, "Thank you."

"Just don't tell anyone who I am."

Ralph asked, "Were you in that tree watching us when we were talking to Benjamin?"

Peppy smiled and said, "That would be telling if I said I was."

"You need to keep an eye on the Chief of Police Steven."

"Someone is out to kill you two and I am gonna make sure that you guys get home safely. Then I am going to do some snooping around Chief Steven's home."

"Just watch your butt."

"Now that's gonna be hard to do without eyes in the back of my head."

At the cabin, Ralph bid goodbye to the Green Shadow and watched her fly skyward. Ralph then inquired, "Are you alright Tara?"

"No. I just had the thought that Vic, Bess, and Peppy are in trouble."

"Let's go see."

Tara hooked her arms under Ralph's shoulders and flew off.

Ralph slowly opened the door to Bess's home and asked, "Anyone to home?" Ralph looked back at Tara and said, "I don't like this. Grab a club and be ready for anything. You check the kitchen, and I check the rest of the house."

Ralph entered the living room with the curtains torn down and smashed furniture and upside down. Tara shouted from the kitchen, "Come here quick!"

Ralph found Tara on the floor holding the bloodied, lifeless body of Bess and Tara said, "Vic is over there."

"Where is Tisha?"

"Over here," groaned Tisha from under an over turned sofa.

Ralph stated, "Call the police while I check the rest of the house."

Minutes later, Ralph put an unconscious, badly beaten Peppy on the floor in the living room. Wiped the green makeup off her and had Tara change her clothes so no one would now that she was the Valley's Green Shadow.

The paramedics arrived first and tried to revive Bess and her husband but couldn't. Peppy opened her eyes and asked, "How's mom and Dad? Are they alright?"

Tara shook her head saying, "I am sorry."

Peppy cried on Tara's shoulder for a minute then said, "I followed the Chief of police here and tried to stop him but he had something called a taser, that knocked me out."

"Do you know what he wanted?"

"He wanted to kill you two."

Ralph stated, "Tara we have to get to the lockup right now. Peppy, you stay here with Tisha."

"No! I want Chief Steven's head! Oh, thanks for hiding who I am."

The police slowly entered and asked, "Human, do you know what happened here?"

"Yeah. Your chief went nuts. Now, if you will excuse me, my wife and I have to get to the lockup."

"You can't accuse Chief Steven without positive proof."

Peppy glowered, "I'm all the proof Ralph needs because I saw Chief Steven bet my parents to death before he used that thing on me!"

"What were they looking for?"

"Us," stated Ralph.

Tara ordered, "Preppy, you have to stay here and help the police."

"I'm coming with you."

"Alright you can come. Tisha, see if you can clean things up."

At the lockup, Ralph Tara and Peppy found the guard behind the desk dead with burn marks to his neck.

Peppy rushed in Franks cell and found him on the floor with an arrow in his stomach.

Tara shouted, "Kathleen is gone!"

Without warning, five police officers rushed in, pointed their crossbows at Ralph, Tara, and Peppy hollering, "No one move!"

Peppy stated, "If you check the computer play back you will see who did this."

One of the Pixie Police then stated, "Put an A-P-B out on the human female and Chief Steven."

Chapter 19

KIDNAPPED

Outside the lockup, Tara suggested, "Ralph. With Peppy's parents' dead, why can't she stay with us for a few weeks."

Ralph said, "Of course you know Kathleen will go after Peppy and kill her just for spite?" Ralph then whispered, "One more thing, aren't you worried that Peppy will start flirting with me?"

"If you do anything foolish with Peppy I will make sure it never happened again."

At the cabin, Peppy checked the place to make sure that everything was clear. Then she sat in a wicker chair with a crossbow in her lap to keep guard.

The next morning, Ralph woke, rolled on his right side to say good-morning to his wife. But was surprised to see an unresponsive Peppy in bed with him and a note on her chest. That read; if this is the best you have, I win. P-S if you want to see Tara again, tell me where she keeps her drugs. Affectionately yours, Kathleen.

Ralph shook Peppy to wake her but couldn't, he slapped her in the face several times to wake her but there was no response. Ralph picked up Peppy, carried her to the outside shower, held her around the waist and turned on the water. He then shook Peppy saying, "Come on, show some signs of life."

After three minutes of trying to wake Peppy, the lethargic Pixie placed her hands-on Ralph's bare chest saying, "It's too early to get up, mom."

"Come on Peppy, snap out of it will ya!"

Peppy then moaned, "Pete you can't be in the shower with me, Dad will kill you if he finds out. So, get out, get out." and began to holler as she beat Ralph's chest.

Ralph shook Peppy again saying, "Snap out of it Peppy, will ya!"

Peppy opened her eyes, stared at Ralph, and hollered, "Ohmigosh! I don't think we shouldn't be doing this! Tara will catch us."

"Sorry I didn't have time to dress us, Tara is missing, and I could not wake you so I brought you in the shower to revive you." As soon as Ralph let Peppy go, her knees buckled, he grabbed her and held her close to him. She looked up, smiled, and said, "My legs feel like rubber."

"Hold on to the side of the shower stall until your legs regain their strength and can you tell me what happened to Tara?"

Peppy stared at Ralph and giggled and said, "I don't believe that I'm in the shower with you in my undies." He slapped her in the face again saying, "Come to your senses girl! This is not funny, Tara is missing and all you can do is laugh?"

"Sorry. Give me a few minutes to clear my head." Peppy let go of the side of the shower and almost fell again. She looked down, then stated, "This is a fine how do you do. I get you right where I wanted you and I can't do anything, so you might as well hand me a towel from over there?" Peppy let go of the side of the shower stall to take the towel and fell against Ralph. He held her saying, "I am not hinting that we mate, I am just going to carry you inside and put you on the couch."

"Could you at least put a towel over me."

"If I let go, you will do a face plant on the shower floor."

"Carry away."

Ralph placed Peppy on the couch, covered her, sat on the edge and Peppy asked, "Could you rub my back? It hurts really bad."

"Peppy M. Morass, I know what you want and it is not going to happen. Now, let me get dressed so I can make us some breakfast."

"All I wanted you to do is rub my back. Please!"

Ralph sighed, and said, "Okay roll over on your stomach." He then asked, "Where did you get those red marks on your back from? Never mind, stay right there while I get the ointment."

"Well Duh! Where do you think I am going to go?"

While Ralph was rubbing the cream on Peppy's back she stated, "All I can remember is waking up tied to a tree face first, with Kathleen and Chief Steven behind me. Kathleen asked me where Tara's drugs were. When I told her that I didn't know, Chief Steven, pressed something against my back that sting something fierce. After a few minutes of that torture, I passed out. I remember hearing Kathleen say something about my clothes and a bed. Do you suppose the Chief?"

Ralph interrupted and said, "Kathleen would not have permitted it."

"Anyways when I came too again, Chief Steven sprayed me in the face with something that smelled like lilac saying, goodbye. The next thing I remember opening my eyes in the shower with you."

"Who is this Pete fella?"

"Who told you about Pete?" questioned a nervous Peppy.

"You did when we were in the shower."

"He is the only guy that saw me in my altogether, outside of you. I had just finished school. Mom and Dad were gone for the day so I decided to take a shower before I did the town with Pete. While I was showering he came over and boldly walked in on me. I tried to cover myself when he pulled back the curtain, smiled at me and said, "Looking good. Forget about doing the town," sat on the commode to undressed. As I watched him unbutton his shirt, all I could think of was being pregnant with his son for nine months. So, I pointed the shower nozzle at him and sprayed him in the face telling him that it wasn't right for him to be in the bathroom with me and that he should leave. He shouted, "Alright for you!" and stormed out off.

"Are you telling me the truth this time?"

"Yes, and my thighs up to my hips hurt real bad. Can you rub them to?"

"You're pushing it Peppy, but okay."

After, Peppy rolled on her back and said, "Yes, and thank you, I feels a lot better, now how about a kiss?"

"I think you need a cold shower."

"I think you should put something on before you make breakfast."

A dressed Ralph made breakfast, placed a white round table on the front porch with two chairs, he then hung a hammock.

While Ralph was eating his bacon and eggs, Peppy, clad in her pink underwear, put her plate of food on the table, sat down and said, "So, what are we going to do about the sleeping arrangement?"

"Peppy what does the Word of God say about how a woman should dress?"

"A woman should adorn herself in modest, respectable, apparel so it does not entice a man. In other words, we should dress as if Christ is our escort."

"What you are wearing right now, is it modest clothing?" asked Ralph

"I figure since we are good friends, it's alright for us to see each other in our underwear."

"It would be fine if I was a female, but I am not. I tell you what, you can walk around inside the cabin any way you like as long as I am outside. Just let me know, so I don't walk in on you."

"Deal." Peppy thought for a minute then asked, "What will you do if Kathleen kills Tara?"

"Bring Kathleen to justice then look for a new wife." Ralph smiled, placed his hand on top of Peppy's and said, "Get dressed in your green outfit so we can find Tara."

Peppy stared at Ralph's hand on hers, smiled thinking, "By putting his hand on mine while he is smiling, he just gave me the guarantee that if Tara dies, I am going to his mate. Yes!"

Ralph then stated, "Concerning the sleeping arrangements. Peppy you sleep in the bed in the cabin and I'll sleep in the hammock."

"I don't want to push you out of your home."

"I like sleeping outside. Now get ready."

When Peppy saw Clint wave as he walked up the path. An embarrass Peppy squealed as she sprang out of her seat and darted inside. Clint sat at the table and said, "There is a rumor going around that you kicked Tara out because you wanted Peppy, so Tara killed Peppy in revenge. Now, who was that young thing that ran in the cabin in her undies?"

Peppy exited the cabin clad in jeans and a long sleeve green top saying, "I am not dead and Ralph didn't get rid of Tara for me. She was kidnapped by Kathleen and Police Chief Steven and no, I wasn't out here in my unmentionables. I swear you men have a one-track mind. Ralph, I'm gonna do some snooping around see you tonight."

Clint watched Peppy fly away and stated "I have to admit she is a cute one. But why would the human called Kathleen, kidnap your mate? It doesn't make sense."

"Kathleen and the ones who work at Specialty Lab want Tara's drugs and will stop at nothing to get it. Because, for some reason the lab wants Pixies and Tara's drugs."

"Is that why my sister Bess, and her husband were murdered?"

"The Chief and Kathleen were looking for me and Tara and tried to beat the information out of them. By the way, do you know if the police chief has a private cabin somewhere?"

Clint thought for a minute then stated, "All I know is that the Police Chief lives too high on the hog for what the valley pays him. But there is gossip going around that the white house on the southern ridge belongs to him. However, the only way up there is to fly. Well, I got to go and say hi to that cute pixie for me. Oh, I should tell you I stashed some climbing gear underneath the bed talk to you later."

In town, Ralph sat drinking his coffee in the outside café staring up at a white spot on the South Ridge and thought, *"That has to be the place."*

After a 5-mile trek through the swamp, Ralph reached the base of the cliff, looked up at the 1500-foot cliff and, muttered, "I am not a mountain climber but if I want to Tara back I have to learn real fast."

An hour later, Ralph made it to the top, looked over the edge and stated, "That is a long way down."

Once Ralph made the three-mile trek through the woods he came to a white mansion that resembled the Greek Parthenon. The chief of police greeted him and said, "You are right on time." he brought Ralph to a large swimming pool that was surrounded by Greek statues. Kathleen walked up to him, clad in a deep blue bikini, smiled and, asked, "You come for the party tonight? Oh, that's right you're missing someone you love. Just give me what I want and you can have her back."

Ralph grabbed Kathleen by her shoulders and hollered. "What have you done with Tara?"

Steven stated, "I wouldn't do that if I were you because right now, three dozen of my men have their crossbows pointed at your head so let her go, or you're a dead man."

Ralph smiled devilishly, grab Kathleen, spun her around put his arm around her throat and said, "Tell me where Tara is and I'll let her go."

Steven replied your mate is somewhere safe and she won't be harmed if you give Kathleen the drugs."

Ralph eyed Tara's wedding ring on a small white square table next to a beige recliner. He smiled diabolically, grabbed the bottom of Kathleen's bikini and pulled up, giving her a super wedge before shoving her in the pool.

Kathleen's surfaced, held onto the edge of the pool and screamed, "Don't let him escape!"

Steven grabbed Ralph and ordered, "Get off my property before I have you shot."

Ralph shoved Steven in the pool saying, "Get out of my face you bag of wind." He then helped Kathleen out of the pool and stated, "I'll give you one last chance to stop what you're doing and repent."

"For what?"

Ralph pushed Kathleen back in the pool as Steven climbed out, clapped his hands. Two muscle bound male pixies, dressed in black, grabbed Ralph by his arms. Steven said, "If specialty labs didn't need you to get the drugs I would have you thrown off the cliff. You have just two weeks to hand over those drugs or I will deliver Tara back to you in a box of pine."

The two muscular pixies took flight with Ralph, landed at the base of the cliff with him and instructed, "You show your face around Mister Steven's place without the drugs it will be your last."

Ralph watched the pixies fly away and moaned, "At least they could have done was bring me to the other side of the swamp."

"Say please."

Ralph turned around and saw Peppy all decked out in green and asked, "How long have you been standing there?"

"Long enough. You have any luck with Chief Steven?"

"I saw Tara's wedding ring on a table by the pool so he is holding her somewhere on his property. What I want you to do is go to my place and bring Tara's security guards here."

"Are we going to rescue Tara?"

"Yes. Tell the security team that I want them to be armed with plenty of sleeping darts. But first, you are going to carry me across this swamp."

Peppy stood behind Ralph, put her arms around him then groaned as her wings buzzed.

Ralph inquired, "How come we are still on the ground?"

Peppy snickered, "You are one heavy dude."

"Stop horsing around and let's go!"

On the other side of the swamp, Peppy gave Ralph a kiss and said, "I'll be back shortly."

Back at the sidewalk cafe, Ralph drew a sketch of Steven's property and the surrounding area. Two male Pixies sat at his table with him and one said, "Hey, Andy, isn't this the human that murdered that older couple?"

"Sure, is What do you say we teach him a lesson that he will never forget."

Susan from the hospital approached the two and said, "Why pound the snot out of him when you can have fun with me."

Andy grabbed Susan around her waist and tried to kiss her. She quickly brought her knee up sending him on his knees in great pain. The other tried to attack her but she landed a powerful roundhouse kick to his face that knocked him out. As Andy was standing, Susan broke a chair over his back. She then shouted, "Get out of here before I lose my temper!" Susan grabbed Ralph's right shoulder and asked, "Are you alright?"

"Yeah and thanks. Where did you learn to fight like that?"

"I've been taking self-defense lessons."

"I'm planning a raid on police chief Steven's hideaway. You want in?"

"If it includes the humans that put me in that cage, just try and keep me away."

Chapter 20

PLANS GONE WRONG

Early the next morning, Ralph awoke to someone pounding on the front door. A blurry eyed Ralph half-heartedly dawn his robe, opened the door saw Peppy and Tara's security team and asked, "Do you guys know what time it is?"

Missy snickered and stated, "Peekaboo, I see a pair good looking legs."

Ralph quickly closed his robe and said. "Come on in. I suppose you want breakfast."

Peppy approached Ralph, closed his robe properly, whispered. "Mama's gotta take care of her promised man."

"You might wind up disappointed when Tara comes back."

"No matter what the outcome will be, I'm loving every minute of it."

Missy announced, "Listen up everyone! After breakfast, we set up camp in the back and the bathroom is outside."

While Misty, Ditsy, and Mitty were setting up camp, Missy sat at the table with Ralph and inquired, "What's your plan of attack?"

This is the layout of Chief Steven's place; first thing tomorrow morning, have your ladies build a mock structure, and pool area of Steven's place. Then where I have a circle, erect a dummy guard. I want this attack to go like clockwork." Ralph turned to Peppy and said, "Go get Susan and bring her here."

After the second practice attack, Missy shouted, "Fall in on the double!" She stood in front of the security squad and hollered, "Peppy and Susan, you were the only two that knew what they were doing! Ditsy, what were you doing with that guard? Making friends with it? It should have taken you that long to immobilizes him and move on. A second longer and he will have his knife in your chest. Mitty and Misty, what were you two doing around the pool era, having a tea party?"

Mitty replied, "Pool, what pool? All I saw were a bunch of rocks in a circle."

"If that's what you think, then during the raid on Chief Steven's home you will be the first to be taken out! Okay, ladies, let's do it again and this time, try and get it right!"

Nine that night Missy shouted, "That's it for day one ladies. We start right after breakfast tomorrow!"

Peppy joined Ralph on the front porch and inquired, "How are you doing?"

"Bushed, but it will be worth it when I have Tara back."

"Ditsy is going to make a sandwich run. Do you want anything?"

"No, I'm fine."

"You have to eat something so you will have your strength for the attack."

"Alright give me a steak and cheese Hoagie."

"Good, I'll tell her." Peppy returned two minutes later, and instructed, "Ralph, take off your shirt and loosen your knickers then lie on the Hammock. I want to give you a back rub that you will never forget."

"How about if I just take off my shirt?"

"That will work."

The next thing Ralph knew Peppy was telling him that the food had arrived. Ralph then noticed that his pants were opened but never said anything to Peppy. When she walked up to him, rested her hand on his shoulder saying, "I had to loosen your belt so I could take care of that nasty scrape just above your tailbone."

"I appreciate your concern, but, please ask next time."

"You don't have to be a prude around me. It's my job as a female pixie to take care of your needs."

The day of the raid on Chief's Steven's home, a leprechaun boldly walked up to Ralph stuck up his hand saying, "Hi, I'm Patrick Seamus,

Fionn Oisin Colm O'Donnagái O'Brien. I heard that you are having problems with humans, experimenting on sprites."

"We are about to launch a raid on the snitch that has my wife captive. Care to join us?"

"I wouldn't miss it."

"Let me get you a crossbow."

"Don't need one." Patrick quickly rubbed his hands together and stretched them out in front of him, sending a charge of lightning from his fingers that shattered a small tree."

"Impressive. You are in."

At the base of the cliff, Missy stated, "Ditsy, Misty, you take the right flank Susan and Peppy take the left. Mitty, and I will cover the rear. Ralph and Patrick, you two attack the front. Just remember, no one moves until I give the signal."

Exactly at eight that morning, Missy gave the go ahead. The group assented to the top of the cliff. Patrick let go a charge of lightning from his fingers that shattered the Chief's front door. and shouted, "Ralph, I'll take care of the ones outside, you go rescue your wife!"

Ralph charged inside then up the stairs to check the rooms which were empty. But when he opened the bathroom door he found Kathleen soaking in a bathtub full of suds. She smiled at him and said, "Don't you know that it is not polite to barge in the bathroom when a lady is in the tub."

"I know, but you are no lady. Now, where is my wife? And pointed his crossbow at her.

"You wouldn't shoot me, would you?"

Ralph asked again, "Where is Tara?"

Kathleen grabbed a towel, slowly stood, as she stated, "I don't know. What did she do? take off on you."

Ralph hesitated to shoot and was kicked in the stomach by Kathleen as she darted out the door to make her escape. Ralph rolled over on the floor and fired a dart at Kathleen. She screamed as grabbed her shoulder and tumbled down the stairs. But when Ralph got there all he found was a small pool of blood. Patrick raced up to him and said, "I am sorry a pixie guard took off with Kathleen." Ralph shouted, "Pat, Duck!" and shot a Chief Steven's guards as he entered the front door.

Patrick pointed to Steven outside trying to sneak into the woods. Ralph hollered, "Freeze Creep!"

Pixie, Chief Steven jumped off the cliff to fly away, Ralph fired a dart that struck him between his shoulder blades, disabling his wings. Steven screamed as he plummeted to his death.

Missy walked up to Ralph and reported, "All clear outside. But we haven't found Steven yet."

"I did. He tried to escape so I shot him and he splattered on the rocks at the base of the cleft. Spread out and search every room for Tara. I'll take the basement."

"Did you find Kathleen?"

"Yeah, in the bathtub. But She got away."

"In other words, she flaunted what she had, at you as a means to distraction, you fell for it and she escaped."

"No comment."

"In the dark basement full of cobwebs, Ralph passed old furniture, and unopened wooden containers. Then in the far back right corner, Ralph entered a cage with straw on the floor and shackles attached to the wall. He chased a rat away from a metal plate with half eaten food and knew Tara was there.

Peppy walked in the cage and asked, "Did you find her?"

"We were too late, he moved her before we got here."

Peppy pointed to some scribbling on the wall and asked, "What is that?"

Ralph read, "I am glad you were in the lab the day I met you, T... Tears filled Ralph's eyes and he collared in the straw trying to hold back his emotions. Peppy sat next to him and stated tenderly, "We'll find her. Now how about a hug?"

Some time later, Peppy stood, with a smile and said, "Whoa. That was more than a hug. But, I am not complaining."

"I am sorry I lost control of my emotions. Let me clean the straw off your clothes so people won't think that we were romping in the hay."

"Didn't we?" asked a puzzled Peppy.

"No, we didn't. I just responded to your tenderness that's all. But, we never mated."

"Could have fooled me."

"Alright, so I caved under the pressure a little because we haven't found Tara and I allowed my passion to get the best of me."

"Relax. I'm just giving you a hard time that's all." Peppy put her finger to Ralph's lips, smiled and whispered, "Shhhh. I am just glad I was around to help you in your time of need, and it will be the smile on your face that Tara won't understand."

"Thank you."

Missy suddenly walked in the cage and said, "There you two are. We are all set to go. The police carted off Steven's thugs." She quickly glanced around and asked, "Have you found Tara?"

"No. They moved her before we got here. What do you say we find some swimsuits, make good use of the pool and the enjoy the food in the fridge before we go?"

At the pool side, Ditsy clad in a Topaz, one-piece bathing suit, approached Ralph relaxing in a lounge chair and asked, "Aren't you coming in?"

"No, I just want to relax and be quiet for now." Ralph glanced at Patrick and inquired, "What's bothering you?"

"This raid was too easy. It is almost as if Steven wanted us to stay." Patrick then shouted, "It's a trap! Ladies, leave your gear and fly as fast as you can!"

Ditsy grabbed Patrick by his arms, Susan picked up Ralph and flew after Tara's security team. Fifty feet from the house, it exploded in a ball of fire, that sent everyone spiraling downward out of control. Minutes later, Missy surfaced in the swamp and shouted, "I need a head count!"

Susan shouted, "Sue here with Ralph."

Misty hollered, "I'm in one piece with Peppy."

Mitty moaned, "I'm alive, I think!"

"Ditsy report! Anyone see Ditsy?"

Ditsy caught several times and said, "Ditsy here with Patrick."

Back at the cabin, Missy had everyone stand in formation and growled, "Alright you bunch of losers. Which one of you blew it by telling Steven that we were coming?"

"I don't understand," questioned Mitty.

"One of you gave away our position to Steven's guards."

Ralph touched Missy's shoulder and said, "It's no one's fault. Steven must have figured that I would do something like this after I paid him a visit." Ralph took Missy aside and said, "Don't be so hard on your girls. They did their best."

"How can you say that when we didn't find Tara."

"We did catch Specialty Lab's informer. Unfortunately, Kathleen got away."

Peppy approached Ralph in a bathing suit holding a bath towel, and bottle of rubbing liniment and stated firmly, "Go in the bedroom take everything off, put the towel on and call me when you are ready."

"Ready for what?"

"Your rubdown. Now go!"

A discouraged Ralph stated, "I don't need the towel for you to give me a body rub."

In the bedroom, Peppy stared at Ralph on his stomach on the bed, folded his clothes. Then poured some liniment in her hands and began to rub Ralph's thighs and inquired, "Why so down in the mouth?"

"I don't think we will find Tara alive."

"You have to have faith that you will be reunited with your wife." Peppy then stated, "That scrape on your tailbone doesn't look to good and where did you get that nasty looking cut on your tushy? I'll be right back with some antibiotic cream and gauze."

With the wounds taken care of, Peppy began to rub Ralph's shoulders and back and questioned, "Did you really mean it when you told me that you would mate with me if something happened to Tara? Ralph, are you listening to me?"

Peppy covered Ralph with a bed sheet, went to snuggle with him but thought, "I better not. Things might happen."

The next morning, the Mayer of Little Ireland pounded on cabin door. Ralph opened it and asked, "What can I do for you, Sir?"

The Mayer roared, "Who gave you the authority to raid Police Chief Steven's summer home?"

"I didn't know I needed permission to take out a murder."

"The Police Chief was an upstanding citizen of this community and you and your gang of thugs killed him in cold blood."

Susan handed the Mayor a note book and said, "I took this from the Chief's desk. It is a journal of his dealings with Specialty Labs."

"That doesn't give you and your thugs the right to take the law into your own hands."

Susan smiled and inquired, "Mayor. How is Miss Candy doing? Did that micro bikini you bought her fit?"

"On second thought Ralph my boy, you should be commended for your actions."

"You can keep your medals and the phony praise Mayor. I just want my wife back."

"With the Mayor gone, Ralph stated, "It is time to go home. Peppy can you fetch Tisha?"

That night, while everyone was sleeping, Ralph sat on the front porch staring at the few stars through the trees. Thinking about his wife and where she was. Peppy sat beside him, held his arm saying, "Don't worry we will find her."

"Thank you. Your support means a lot to me. Join me in the hammock?"

"Wouldn't mind if I kept you company tonight? I guess you need it right now."

In the morning, Ralph found a note on the table that read, "Meet me at the sidewalk cafe at ten AM and come alone. Affectionately Kathleen."

He gave Peppy a peck on her cheek saying, "Tell everyone to hold off on going home until I get back."

"I'm coming with you."

"No. I want you to stay here and get Tisha."

Ralph sat at a sidewalk cafe table, a short, cute pixie waitress clad in a black and white dress greeted him with a smile and asked, "You're human aren't you?"

"Yes, ma'am I am."

"Can I shake your hand? I never touched a human before."

Ralph shook her hand saying, "Give me a cup of coffee, and an egg sandwich."

The waitress walked away staring at her hand amazed that she accurately touched a human.

Later, as Ralph was enjoying his coffee and egg, he glanced up at a tree and saw a faint outline of somebody perched in it. Kathleen promptly sat at the table across from him wearing a low-cut red dress and said, "You're looking good today."

"Can the pleasantries Kathleen, what do you want?"

"Your little raid on Steven's cliff home didn't change things. I still want Tara's drugs."

"Why don't you ask her?"

"I have and she will not talk."

"Then, how do you expect me to tell you when Tara never told me where the drugs were herself."

"Don't play games with me, Ralph. Because you will lose."

"Why do you want the drugs? They're no good to humans. You would have to use a powerful magnifying glass to mix the ingredient just right."

"Then give me the book along with the drugs."

"There isn't a book. The knowledge is passed on down by word of mouth."

Kathleen's face grew dark as she growled, "I am warning you, Ralph. If you, don't give me what I want, I will send Tara back to you piece by piece."

Ralph's countenance softened and stated, "Do you remember when we first met? You were so innocent and would giggle every time I kissed you."

Kathleen smiled and said, "I felt like I was doing something naughty when we kissed. Hey, do you remember when I made that seven-layer chocolate cake for you?"

"How could I forget. You tripped and the cake landed in my face."

Kathleen laughed, "At least the pieces we salvaged were good."

"Do you remember what we use to do in church?"

"Sure do. We would hold hands all through the service. I would hold the hymnal in my left hand and you would turn the pages with your left."

After you asked me to marry you, I went home that night and wrote the plans for our wedding."

Ralph tone of voice changed so serious and said, "Shortly after you took a job a Specially Labs you changed and started to go to bed with the boss. Why?"

"It was two week after I began to work there. Stan invited me to his home for dinner. The next morning, I woke in bed with him, and wondered how I was going to tell you that I was forced into doing something I didn't want to. Hey! That's none of your business! You have three weeks to hand over the drugs, or Tara dies!" Kathleen then stormed off.

Chapter 21

BUGGED

As Ralph was walking back to the cabin, he paused and said, "Alright Peppy you can stop following me. The threat of Kathleen and her cohorts abducting me is passed."

A green Peppy flew down from a nearby tree and asked, "How did you know it was me?"

"You have a unique ability to blend in with the background I admit. But I know you like a well read book."

"Dang, I guess I have to keep trying. Where to from here?"

"Did you get Tisha?"

"Misty went for her and what's bugging you?"

"Tara's message on the wall. I wasn't in the lab the day we met Tara. I was in the garden and she flew into me."

"Do you suppose they are keeping Tara in the lab?" Ralph thought for a minute then said, "Kathleen had on her favorite red dress and if I remember correctly her friend Sally still has it."

"Maybe it was another red dress."

"It's the same low-cut red dress because Kathleen had a fancy red 'K' embroidered just below the left shoulder. Which means Kathleen was at the Lab."

"Earth to Ralph, Earth to Ralph. Kathy is only twelve inches tall and so are you. So, it could not have been the same dress. She is messing with your mind. But, you may be right about Tara being held in the lab."

"If I know Kathleen, she found a way to make herself big again."

"There is still something bothering you."

"I told Kathleen that she had changed once she took a job at the lab. She replied, I woke up in bed with Stan the next morning. Do you suppose Stan is blackmailing Kathleen?"

Back at the cabin, Ralph approached Tisha in the outside shower and said, "When we get back home. I will need you to do a few more favors for me."

"As long as I am part of the action this time. Now can you hand me my towel?"

"You're in and I don't see any towel."

"Don't say that."

"Just kidding."

In the basement of Ralph's home, he started at Peppy, Susan, and the security team and asked, "Am I going to be a foot tall for the rest of my life?"

Peppy stated. "The effects of Little Ireland should wear off in a day or two. Until then, relax."

"That's easy for you to say. You are not going to be the one who will be embarrassed when it happens."

Peppy put her hand on her mouth, giggled then said, "We won't look when that happens."

"Yeah, I bet. Tisha, put some clothes in a box under that bush. When I sneeze three times, I'll make a dash for it so I'm not exposed. Peppy, go upstairs and get Muf-Muf from the fireplace mantle."

"I don't think I can do that being a foot tall."

Five minutes later, Peppy dropped the Pixie doll at Ralph's feet. He ordered, "Get its clothes off."

Susan stared at Ralph fondling a nude Muf-Muf and asked, "Why are you getting fresh with that pixie doll?"

"There is a reason why Kathleen kept putting this stupid doll near me whenever she left. I was hoping to find a hidden mic inside of it. But, I guess I was wrong."

Ditsy carefully studied Muf-Muf, noticed scrapes on the inside of her knees and on the side of her ribs. Then stated, "Mitty. Susan, bend the dolls legs until her knees are touching Muf-Muf's side. Good, now bend the legs at the knees. You should yeah a click."

The front half of Muf-Muf's torsos and face sprang off. Ralph muttered, "I knew it! It's a listening device with a miniature surveillance camera. No doubt it's linked to my Wi-Fi."

Ditsy took a closer look and whispered, "Shhh. No one talks until I dismantle it."

Missy showed Ralph the knapsack that Tara had the black powder in and said, "Someone's been in this. When we left it was almost three quarters full. Now, look at it."

"Kathleen must have gotten in my house somehow and used it to enlarge herself."

That evening, Ralph was his normal size, Kathleen strolled in and said, "Hi Love. Meet any cute Pixies lately?"

"You have a lot of nerve coming in my home after what you've done. Now leave."

"Did you forget that you can't throw me out. Oh, you can throw me out but, I can also take you to court and have them force you into submission. Then I'll tell the media about the women you have living in your basement."

"They are Pixies and there is a difference you know."

"Did you know that the lab discovered that there is no difference between a Pixie's physiology and a human."

Ralph walked up to Kathleen, handed Muf-Muf to her and said, "Here is your doll minus the surveillance equipment that was inside it. Now get out!"

Kathleen put the doll down and questioned, "Don't you want to know where your sweet little Tara is?" She then began to get ready to take a shower. Ralph stopped her and forcefully escorted her to the front door. Kathleen jabbed Ralph between his pockets sending him down on his knees in pain, walked by him saying, "If you want me I'll be in the shower."

Missy had her security team hovering in the hall and she said, "Not one step further, Miss Bug Nuggets."

"Out of my way insects or I'll swat you!"

Peppy flew behind Kathleen holding a steak knife in her hand, hovered then flew as fast as she could and rammed the knife in Kathleen's upper thigh. She screamed as she fell to the floor trying to pull the knife out.

Peppy quickly took another steak knife from the drawer, flew to where Kathleen was and was about to drive that knife in her chest. Ralph caught Peppy saying, "Oh no you don't. Pixie's don't kill people no matter how evil they are."

Ralph knelt by Kathleen, removed the knife, and asked, "What power does Stan hold over you that you are willing to kill a Pixie?"

"I can't tell you."

Ralph held Peppy as she screamed and buzzed her wings in an effort to attack Kathleen. Kathleen smiled, gently touched his face, and said, "I would like to tell you, but I can't." and looked down at her chest.

With his free hand, Ralph unbuttoned Kathleen's blouse, saw that she was wearing a wire. Kathleen took a pen in her hand and wrote on Ralph's arm, basement far left. Top cage. then left.

Ralph held Peppy up to his face and said, "Settle down young lady or I will turn you over my knee and paddle your bare bottom."

"You wouldn't dare spank a grown Pixie."

Ralph tugged on Peppy's slacks, she quickly grabbed them by the waistband and said, "Alright, alright, alright. Just don't treat me like a child."

"When you act like a child, I will treat you like one. However, you have to forgive Kathleen. Now give me a hug." Ralph then stated, "Missy, assemble your team and go to the basement lab and check to see if they have Tara locked up in a cage like Kathleen said. But, whatever you do, don't get yourselves caught."

"Why don't you come with us."

"Give me a minute to put on my black jammies."

Peppy looked at what Kathleen wrote on Ralph's arm and said, "I think it is a trap."

"We will just have to take that chance. Oh, ah, Missy are Tara's drugs still in the garage?"

"All the drugs are there from what I can see, but I have no way to get in without the key."

Peppy stated, "If we go to the lab we are all gonna be put in cages for sure. I say we find another way to rescue Tara."

Ralph asked, "Alright Peppy how do you propose we do it?"

"Well we, ah. I don't know. What if we have Tisha Gibson put on hot pants and a halter top and lure the guard away from his post. Then she can use some chloroform to incapacitate him. While she is busy with the guard, I will sneak in and disable the alarm. Then we rescue Tara. Susan, you be the lookout, Missy you have your ladies scattered around the lab just in case of a trap."

That night, Tisha stepped out of Ralph's car grumbling, "I feel absolutely naked in this skimpy getup. What if he wants to handle my merchandise?"

"You'll be fine and he won't."

"Of course, you know after tonight I will no longer have a job here."

"Things will work out for you, now go."

Tisha approached the guard at Specialty labs. Struck a flirtatious pose and asked, "Hey Jack, are you lonely tonight?"

The guard smiled and said, "Tisha. You are looking smashing. But I can't leave my post." he then put his arm around her waist and pulled her close.

Tisha's heart pounded as she took out the gauze pad with the chloroform on it and shoved it in his face. Jack collapsed in Tisha's arms, she whispered, "Somebody help."

Ralph stashed the guard, and Peppy gave the all clear.

In the dim light of the basement Lab, Ralph quickly rushed to Tara's cage and found her unconscious. As he cradled his sweetheart in his arms. Kathleen snapped on the lights and said, "Guards, arrest that man for trying to steal one of the lab's projects."

The guard was about to put the handcuffs on Ralph when Ditsy shot him with a sedative dart. Ralph walked up to Kathleen and asked, "You wanna tell me why you turned your back on me?"

"I never stopped loving you even when you hooked up with Tara."

Ralph ripped open Kathleen's blouse, destroyed the wire she was wearing, then said, "Now, you can talk freely."

Tears filled Kathleen's eyes as she stated, "I can't go anywhere without Stan watching me in some way. In the back room, there are twelve Pixies in cages, and the remains of I don't know how many more. Get them out of here before Stan finds you."

Ralph ordered, Peppy, "Have Missy and her team take care of the pixies."

Kathleen then stated, "Hurry, Stan will be here any minute wondering what happened to the wire."

Ralph stared at Kathleen with her blouse open, saw a huge bruise on her rib cage and inquired, "Has Stan been beating you?"

"Yes. Every time I botch a mission he punish me. Now, go before he gets here."

"I take it you came over last night because I busted his surveillance equipment. Then when I would not let you stay in my house Stan beat you."

"That's only the half of it. He threatened to kill my mom if I don't do what he says."

"Why does Stan want Tara, her drugs, and experiment on the Pixies?"

"Stan wants the drugs so he can use someone to sneak in a lab and spy on what they are doing, and he needs Tara to teach him how to use the drugs."

"In other words, if he wants to dispose of someone he hates, shrink them then flush them."

"Exactly. He wants the Pixies to test the drug formula Tara told her. Now, get out of here before Stan come in and finds you."

Ralph went in the back room to make sure all the pixies were gone when Stan walked in. Kathleen reported, "Ralph and his Pixies friends were here and took Tara and the Pixies you had locked up in the back room."

"You idiot!" screamed Stan, then back handed her. Stan then said, "I told you to kill Ralph and cage his pixies! But you couldn't even do that right!" Stan then shoved Kathleen sending her into a rack of empty cages. As soon as she stood, Stan belted her in the stomach as hard as he could. Then whispered, "You are going to Ralph's place and get Tara back or I will kill you and your mom. Now, get out of my sight, you worthless piece of garbage!" then gave Kathleen a shove sending into a metal rack that had long sharp points. One point jabbed her stomach, one pierced her thigh and another went through her chest. Ralph landed a right cross to Stan's jaw, grabbed Kathleen, and dragged her to the elevator.

In the elevator, Kathleen, prayed, "Lord forgive me. I am so sorry for listening to Stan and allowing myself to get tangled up with him. Ralph, please don't let Stan hurt my mom."

"Hold on Kathleen, help will be here shortly."

Back home, Ralph had Susan and Peppy put Tara in her bed, made the 12 Pixies comfortable by the pond, then put the dead Pixie remains in boxes for shipping.

Tisha cleaned up the Pixies they rescued, then fed them with eye dropper before putting them to bed.

Ralph said, "I noticed they all have their wings except that last one."

"That's Beebe with her wings off. Stan decided that removing their wings served no purpose."

"Right now, I need Kathleen's mom's address and phone number. Because Stan is gonna make a play for her."

Chapter 22

KATHLEEN COMES CLEAN

Weeks later, Ralph walked in Kathleen's hospital room, handed Muf-Muf to her and said, "I thought she could keep you company. So, how are you doing?"

Kathleen tucked the doll under the covers next to her and said, "The doctor doesn't understand why I am still alive. Enough about me how is Tara doing?"

"She is in a coma right now and will come out of it soon. But remember, Jesus is the God of the second chance. You are His child and He will not give up on you no matter how bad you screwed up."

"I am so sorry to hear about Tara and will you forgive me for what I did to trick you into getting in bed with me?"

"Sure. No problem."

With tears in her eyes, Kathleen stated, "I am so sorry Ralph that I allowed myself to get mixed up with Stan. But, I didn't tell you the whole truth about what happened between me and him. The second week I worked at the lab, Stan invited me to his place for dinner and told me about his plan to destroy the Pixies and use the ones that were left to serve him. When I refused to go along with his devilish scram, he smiled at me and said, "Oh but you will." When I went to go home, he belted me in the stomach and said, "You are sleeping with me tonight."

"I knew what it meant if I said no, so I let Stan have sex with me that night. I woke in bed with him the next day feeling like I betrayed you, but most of all the Lord." Kathleen broke down and cried, then said, "After, Stan threatened to tell you and the pastor that I was his sex partner if I didn't do what he said. So, to keep me under his thumb, he put a wire on me and sent me to do his dirty work. Frank, his point man went with me everywhere, which meant I had to tend to his daily needs like, body rube and so on. If I said no, I wound up getting a beating from Stan." Kathleen looked away and said, "Years ago I was told by a sister in the Lord that I was called to Minister His Word to the Native Americans. But, because of my dealings with Stan I'm afraid that I blew it Big time."

Ralph said, "Okay Chief Gray Fox you can come in now."

Gray Fox entered, held Kathleen's hand and said, "Your Indian name will be Mourning Dove. With your struggles now in your past, you are the perfect one to minister the Word of God to my people."

"But, I don't have any experience or training."

"What you just went through is what my people need to hear. Say yes, and I'll have you immediately transferred to a hospital near the reservation in Nevada."

Kathleen's face lit up and she said, "Yes! But can I have some time alone with Ralph?"

Alone, Ralph sat on the bed and asked, "What is it that you want?"

"I want you to hold me one last time."

A nurse came in to change Kathleen's dressing and told Ralph that he had to leave. Kathleen stated, "It is alright, he can stay." Kathleen held Ralph's hand while her dressings were being changed, when the nurse left Ralph helped Kathleen put on a new Johnny-coat on then she fell into her arms, saying, "I never stopped loving you." then kissed his lips several times.

Gray Fox came in and Ralph said, "Thank you for protecting Kathleen. Because I wouldn't be surprised if Stan has a hit out on her."

Just then an orderly approached Kathleen's bed saying, "It's time for your shot then took hold of her arm.

Gray Fox took the needle from the orderly, gave it to Ralph then pinned him against the wall with his arm saying, "You're not orderly. Ralph get the security."

With Stan's hit man under arrest, Ralph asked, "How did you know he didn't work in the hospital."

A nurse would have given the injection in the IV not and not her arm. I'll have two of my brave stand guard at her room door until she is transferred."

Kathleen whispered, "Ralph, with the Chief of police dead, me out of commission and Tara missing from the lab. Stan will send some of his men to your place to get Tara. If that fails, he will send some of his men to Little Ireland and take what he wants."

"How did Stan's men know where the valley was?"

"Sorry, Hon. Every night when I was in bed with Stan I had to report to him what went on during the day. Just FYI, you were a lot better than Stan."

At home, Ralph assembled the Pixies and asked, "Which one of you is the fastest?"

Susan raised her hand and said, "I've been clocked at 75 MPH."

"Good, "Go to Little Ireland and tell them to prepare for an all-out attack by Stan's thugs. Then come right back."

"For real?"

"Yes! Now go!"

Ralph called Tisha and said, "I need your assistance one more time. Oh, a friend of mine, Emma needs somebody to buy goods for her business. So, I gave her your name and you report to work in three days with twice the amount Stan was paying you."

"Fantastic, I'll be there in a jiffy."

Tisha walked in the house clad in jeans and a green button-down blouse and asked, "What's up Boss?"

"I need you to help defend my place against Stan's men."

"I'm all yours. Oh, ah, you know what I mean."

Missy reported, "Kathleen's mom is out of town for the week, what do you want me and my girls to do?"

Arm yourselves with arrows, and position yourselves around the outside of the house. Peppy, get Tara and the pixies from the lab and hide them in the mountain caves.

When Susan returned, Ralph told her to hide in the Boston Fern with a cross bow and keep track of what's happens. Ralph threw some pillows on the floor by the fireplace, put on some soft music and instructed, "Tisha, put on something sexy then lie down, by the fireplace so we can pretend like we are making out. Ralph took off his shirt and shouted, "Places everyone!" he curled up next to Tisha on the floor in a skirt and blouse, her hair messed up and asked, "Would you mind if I put my arms around you so it looks like we are kissing."

Tisha opened her blouse and said, "Things have to look like we are into things so go ahead, help yourself."

Ralph hesitated to kiss Tisha so she wrapped her arms around his waist pulled him down on top of her and began to kiss him. Tisha then said, "Don't fight me, relax, we have to make this look real. Put your hand on me so it looks like we are into light petting."

A short time later, three men barged into the house, Ralph stopped kissing Tisha and asked, "Gentlemen, what can I do for you?"

"We're here for the Pixies!"

Tisha fixed herself as Ralph said, "Come on in. Oh, that's right you guys are already in, but, there are no Pixies here. Just me and my girl making out on the floor."

Tisha was fixing herself as the leader, Gus, grabbed her by her arm and yanked her to her feet, and demanded, "Give me Tara or your lady friend will have a new smile."

"I told you there are no Pixies in my house. If you don't believe me, search for yourselves."

In the basement, Gus studied the layout and inquired, "If you don't have any Pixies living here. Then what's is all this?"

"Kathleen loves Pixies and so I built this for her."

Gus stated, "Boys, hold Ralph I might as well have some fun with Miss Tisha."

To stall for time, Tisha smiled sheepishly, and said, "Gus, you don't have to force yourself on me. Give me a minute to get ready then I'm all yours." Tisha slowly unzipped the back of her skirt and let it drop to the grass, and took off her top. When the two men holding Ralph slapped their necks as if they were stung. Then collapsed on the grass out cold. Gus shouted, "Hey, what's going on?" His eyes rolled back in his head as he fell to the ground, a sleep.

Missy and her security team appeared, and Missy questioned, "Is everyone alright?"

A relieved Tisha picked up her clothes and stated, "That was too close. Another minute and I would have been in serious trouble."

Ralph grinned at Tisha and stated, "Nice yellow undies."

"Just turn around so I can make myself decent."

Gus's fourth man stepped into view, shoved Ralph into Tisha, who quickly stepped behind Ralph. The forth man then ordered, Missy and her team to stand with Ralph. Saying, "Tell me where are Tara and her drug are, or I start shooting."

Ditsy went to the garage, opened it and said, "Here are the drugs. But, strangely enough, no Tara."

The man bellowed, "You know as well as I do that the drugs are useless without Tara. So, stop stalling!"

"Hey, piece of cake. Here I will show you."

Ditsy took a hand full of white crystals blew it in the man's face."

He inquired, "You are going somewhere with this? Then fall flat on his face unconscious. Ditsy stood on the man's chest and said, "Oh, did I tell you that I'm Tara's drug understudy?"

Tisha looked at Ralph saying, "I need a hug right now."

"But you are in your undies."

"I don't care! Just hold me!"

Ralph put his arms around Tisha and said, "You are trembling. I didn't know you were that scared. I'm sorry."

"I never did anything like that before," Tisha looked up at Ralph and asked, "Can you hold me for a few more minutes?"

After Tisha dressed, Ralph stated, "I have a better idea. Why don't we shrink Gus and his men, put them in the hamster cage? Then hang them over the water to interrogate them."

Ditsy pointed to Tisha and said, "Brew some cinnamon tea, I'll get the right ingredient."

Ditsy gave each man the tea saying, "Tara said that Cinnamon Tea with green herb and the white powder will not make humans' permanently small. It's the powder from the Fire Mushrooms that will permanently shrink them."

Ralph ordered, "Peppy it's safe to bring Tara and the others out." with the four men shrunk while they were still out, Ralph ordered, "Susan, help Mitty, Ditsy and Misty put some clothes on those men."

"Yes, Sir!" stated Susan with a smile.

Tisha rigged the cage so it would float, then tied a cord to a weight and pulley system so when the rope was pulled, the cage went under the water.

Twenty minutes later, the four men came too in the cage, Tisha held the cord saying, "Hi guys. Remember me? The cleaning lady you use to push around? It looks like the shoe is on the other foot now. I am going to ask you some questions and if I don't like your answer, I pull the cord and you guys will go for a swim."

Gus replied, "Miss Tisha. Give us a break. I didn't mean to do those things to you."

"Wrong answer!" Tisha submerged the cage for five seconds, let it up and said, "That, gentlemen was just to show you that I mean what I say. Now, what does Stan plan to do with Little Ireland after he invalids it?"

"Who said Stan was going to invalid the valley?"

"Wrong answer Gus!" Tisha dunked the cage under the water for six seconds. Then said, "That is not what I wanted to hear. Oh, each time you get it wrong, I add a second to your time under water. Now, let's try it again."

"Stan never said anything to us about attacking the valley."

"Wrong answer!" Tisha let the cage surface after seven seconds, and said, "I didn't mention that Little Ireland was in a valley so I know you are lying."

One of the men, Vic spoke and said, "Stan plans to enslave the Pixies in the valley and have them produce the drugs that he wants."

Gus jabbed Vic in his stomach shouting, "Imbecile!" the other three men jumped on Vic began to beat him. Tisha submerged the cage for a good fifteen seconds to break up the fight, then took Vic out of the cage and gave him dry clothes.

With crossbows pointed at Vic, he slowly approached Beebe, and said, "I know it won't bring your wings back, but, I am sorry for what my boss did to you."

Beebe stated, "I am due for a wing graft when I get back home and yes I forgive you. Do you know when Stan plans to attack the valley?"

"Tomorrow at dawn."

Tisha ordered, "Missy, get them out of the cage, put dry clothes on them, and get them ready to be transported to Little Ireland."

Gus broke free and went after Vic to kill him. Nanette, one of the pixies rescued from the lab, screamed, "Get him!" Took flight, tackled Gus, knocking him into the water, then held him under screaming, "I won't let you hurt any more of my friends!"

Ralph hollered, "Nanette, don't do it!"

She dragged Gus out of the water coughing and gasping for air, then said, "I refuse to lower myself to your level." and turned to walk away. Gus grabbed Nanette by her wings and pulled, sending her stumbling backward onto the grass. Tisha hollered, "No!" picked up Gus and threw against the rocks of the mountain, killing him.

The security team quickly surrounded the other three with their crossbows pointed at them, and said, "Missy, give the word and we will perforate their hides."

"No. Give them something to eat, then call Emma and have her send some of her muscular Pixies to take the three of them to the Valley for trial."

Ralph rested his hand on Tisha's shoulder and asked, "Are you finished giving orders?"

"Yeah, sorry I got carried away."

Ralph handed Tisha her clothes and said, "I think you need to put this on."

With Stan's men taken care of, Ralph stated, "It is time to prepare for the battle for Little Ireland."

Nanette looked up at Ralph and stated, "Me and my friends are grateful that you rescued us from the god-awful lab. So, we are ready to fight to stay free."

Ralph stated, "Missy, get them crossbows and then train them. I am going up stairs to rest for a while."

Tisha grabbed Ralph saying, "No you don't. I want in on this fight too."

"There is a 44-Magnum in the cabinet by the washer, arm yourself, and get ready."

Ralph went upstairs, put on his bathing trunks, and relaxed in the Hot tub."

Peppy quietly sat on the edge of the Hot tub in her two-piece bathing suit, watching the bubbled surround Ralph's body thinking about him, she then asked, "Would it be alright if I join you?"

"Come on in. We need to talk."

Peppy sat in a chair in the water specially made for Pixies and reported, "Tara is holding her own right now and playfully she should come out of the coma soon." Peppy thought for a moment then said, "You miss her, don't you?"

"More than words can say."

"If you don't want to fulfill your promise to be my mate, you don't have to."

"I told you that we would be man and Pixie if something happened to Tara and I plan to follow through with it. But, that's not why you came up here."

"I'm scared to death that I might die during the battle tomorrow."

"Have you met Jesus?"

"Oh yes. I also keep all the traditions of the Pixies."

"Does that include the one that says a Pixie chooses a mate by sleeping with them?"

"I haven't done that yet, but if anything happens to Tara I plan to do it with you."

"Peppy, what does the Word of God say about impurity?"

"Dang! You're right. Oh well. I guess that will have to wait until after we are married. Ah, that's if Tara dies. Not that I am wishing evil on her."

"I know. Come over here so I can give you a needed hug."

"Just a short one."

"You don't trust me?"

"No. I don't trust myself. Oh, alright."

Peppy rested on Ralph's chest and went to sleep.

Chapter 23

A TIME TO CELEBRATE

Two hours before the sun was up, Patrick knocked on the front door. A blurry eyed Ralph opened the door and asked, "Do you like to wake people up at this hour of the morning?"

"Why not! it's a wonderful day for a victory over Stan's men. So, let's get things going!"

Ralph yawned, opened the laundry shut, banged on the inside of it with his fist and shouted, "Rise and shine everyone!"

A minute later, 18 weary Pixies flew up and out the laundry shoot. Ditsy grumbled, "Thanks a lot, Ralph! I did have to use the little Pixie's room when I woke, but thanks to you, I don't now!"

"Sorry. We are having sausage, eggs, toasted English Muffins, and coffee."

"Give me a minute to change." muttered Ditsy.

After breakfast, Ralph said, "Peppy, would you mind staying here to look after Tara."

"I would be honored to."

Ralph announced, "Listen up everyone! This is Patrick who will be in charge of this mission!"

The leprechaun stood on a chair and said, "All your arrows will be dipped in deadly poison because no one of Stan's men should be left alive. Because the secret of the valley of the Pixies must maintained!"

Misty suggested, "Why don't we use the black powder to increase our size. That way we can overpower them."

"No. We need the element of surprise because and a small target is harder to hit. So, what are we going to do?"

Everyone shouted, "Keep the Valley secret at all cost!"

"Say it again and only mean it this time!"

"Keep the Valley secret at all costs!" shouted everyone.

In the cave, Patrick ordered, "Scatter yourselves around the walls and get ready to shoot to kill."

Ralph, Tisha, and Patrick stood in front of the entrance to the valley with their guns ready. Six minutes later, five armed men dressed in army fatigues carrying M-16 rifles approached. Ralph leveled his Winchester at the men saying, "Turn yourselves around and forget the valley of Pixies."

The Sargent stated, "We came here to take a valley and that's what we are going to do. So, stand aside before you get yourselves killed."

"You are outnumbered two to one so, leave or die!" shouted Tisha.

"From what I can see it's the other way around. Now, step aside and let us through."

Patrick shouted, "Alright ladies show yourselves to the gentlemen!" Patrick then informed, "Plus, every Pixie in Little Ireland is armed and waiting for you to step through that Curtain of Vines."

"Your idle threats don't bother me so step aside," and pushed his way into the valley. The Sargent then staggered back in the cave with several thousand arrows stuck in him then fell to the ground, dead. Patrick shouted, "Let them have it, girls!"

The cave was suddenly flooded with Pixies firing arrows at the men. Five minutes later, it was over. Their bodies were dumped in a vacant, mine-shaft and Patrick stated, "Ralph, I want to be with you when you take down Stan."

At specialty Laboratories, Ralph, Patrick, and Tisha entered the elevator carrying a blue and white cooler. Opened it and ordered, "Alright girls you all have your instructions. Plant your bomb and report back to the elevator ASAP."

In seconds, 16 pixies carrying high explosives, flew up the elevator shaft. Ralph, Patrick, and Tisha stepped off the elevator, Ralph smiled and said, "Stan, if I were you I wouldn't be celebrating your victory, rather you should be mourning your defeat."

"Why do you say that?"

"Because the men that you sent to invalid Little Ireland are dead."

Upon hearing, small footprints in the doct work Stan glanced at the ceiling and said, "Friends of yours no doubt."

Patrick glanced at his watch and said, "Right about now the last elector static charge has been planted. In approximately ten minutes you and this lab will be a pile of rubble." Susan claimed out of the backpack stood on Tisha's right shoulder, leveled her crossbow at Stan and said, "Thanks to you, I still have nightmares about this place." then let an arrow fly that struck Stan in his neck."

Ralph then stated, "That arrow was dipped in a neurotoxin and right about now you should find it difficult to move." He then said, "Patrick, Tisha, it's time we left. Stan, it's judgment time for you."

As the elevator door was closing, Stan fell to his knees saying, "You can't leave me here to die."

Ralph stopped the door from closing and asked, "How many Pixie have you mutilated in the name of science?"

"I'll get you for this!"

"No, I don't think so."

From a good distance, away Patrick activated the detonator. Blue charges of stat-electricity shot up from the ground, surrounding the lab above for five seconds before a tremendous exploration shook the ground.

As the black smoke rose from the rubble of the lab, the 17 Pixies headed back to their valley and Patrick left for his home. Ralph gave Tisha a goodbye hug saying, "You know where I live so don't be a stranger."

"As long as I don't have to throw myself at some strange man in my underwear I'll be there."

Ralph walked in his home and remarked, "It's sure quiet now that all the Pixies are gone home. Two hands suddenly gripped Ralph's shoulder, and a soft voice said, "I take it everything went according to plan." Ralph spun around and exclaimed, "Tara, you're a live!"

"Of course, I am. Did you think that I was going to leave you in the hands of that hot little Pixie, Peppy?"

"So how long do we have before you shrink?"

Tara stepped out of her dress saying, "Let's forget about time and enjoy each other's company."

Epilogue

Two days later, Tara was still six feet tall and was sunning herself on the back deck with Ralph when she inquired, "I know Peppy had the hots for you, however when I was being held by Kathleen, did you give into her whims when she came on to you?"

"Why would you think that I played around with Peppy?"

"I know Peppy's a cute ways to get you to do things, so, it would have been easy for you to go for it with her."

Feeling interrogated, Ralph stated, "Honest, nothing went on between Peppy and me, Nothing."

"Nothing went on?" questioned Tara. "Would you like to rephrase that statement?"

"Peppy did say something to me about exercising her right as your best friend if something happened to you."

"Which you eagerly agreed to."

"Can we change the subject?"

Tara giggled and said, "Feeling uncomfortable because I'm getting too close to the truth?"

"Tara!" grumbled Ralph.

"Relax, Hon, I'm just playing with your mind. What do you say I make some coffee and we soak in the hot tub?"

Just then, the front doorbell rang, Ralph, opened the door and greeted a tall stout woman with White wavy hair clad in a crimson dress and an older heavy-set man with gray hair dressed in a green striped suit. The man inquired, "Does Tara Jones live here?"

"Come on in," Ralph then shouted, "Tara, it's for you!"

Tara shouted, "Mom, Dad you are alive! Hay I want you to meet my husband Ralph. Hon, this in my dad Karl, and my mom. Tara Senior."

"You did pretty good in getting a human for a mate," stated Karl, "But have you kept up with your training? Never mind answering that."

"Where are you living now Dad?"

"A quiet place by a river. But, there is a problem."

A note from the author

Kathleen is like a lot of us. We start out in Christ with good intentions to follow the narrow path that He has set before us. Then somewhere along the way we lose sight the path and are tangled up in a mess wondering how we got there.

There is a story of a little girl who lived high in the mountains. Every morning she would gaze across the valley at a lovely home with beautiful gold windows and would think how great it would be to live in that house. One morning she made up her mind that she was going to take a trip to the house with the gold windows. When she arrived at the house in the evening she discovered that the windows were only made from glass. But, when she looked across the valley at her own home she saw that they were gold.

The riches of this world can't compare to the blessings he has for you.

Thor is the Galaxy Sentinel, In the Last Warlord

The Vanishing Hero.
Quest, a journey
The Warlords Revenge.
Rampage
River of Fire
Roswell Converts
The Time Shifter
Crimson.
Shroud of Terror
Nightwalker
Return to Roswell
Galaxy Under Siege
The Time Master

Other books that are available

Christian Allegories
Christian Allegories volume 2
The Chronicles of Mike and Heather
Mysterious Journeys
Murder at the Graves Estate.

CPSIA information can be obtained
at www.ICGtesting.com
Printed in the USA
FFOW03n2344170118
44587247-44473FF